Mary Wagner

My Name Is Harlem

This is a work of fiction. Names, characters, places, and incidents either are the product of the author's imagination or are used fictitiously. Any resemblance to actual persons living or dead, events, or locales is entirely coincidental.

chapter 1

"Harlem, Harlem, come on girl get up. You don't want to be late first day of school do you? Now come on girl rise and shine. You've been waiting all summer for today," Belinda said scurrying from the kitchen to the bedroom trying to get her daughter Harlem up for school.

"Ok Mama, I'm coming. Just one more minute," Harlem said in a drowsy voice.

Belinda gets a little louder. "No, No, just get up now. I don't want to hear "just one more minute". Get up now Harlem Rose before I give the birds these luscious blueberry pancakes I just made for you!"

"I'm coming now Mama," Harlem said as she hollered from the bedroom.

Harlem knew when her mother used "Harlem Rose" and a threat to give her favorite pancakes to the birds, she meant business. Harlem jumped out of bed, brushed her teeth, washed her face, got dressed and was in the kitchen before the last pancake was out of the frying pan and in her plate.

The kitchen wasn't far from the small bedroom Harlem shared with her mother. The apartment was small and crowded with a few meager pieces of furniture Belinda purchased from Harry's Secondhand Furniture Store on East, 185th Street, in South Bronx. That apartment was one of the cleanest in the projects and Belinda was rightfully proud of that.

Belinda was a proud woman. Working as an LPN at the local hospital and taking nursing classes at night to become a registered nurse kept her busy and tired, but it gave her life meaning. She knew someday she would be able to leave the projects, move to a nicer apartment and be able to afford to send Harlem to a good college.

Harlem was born on May 1, 1950. Her father, David, was transferred one month later from the army base at Ft. Slocum in New Rochelle, New York to serve with his platoon in Korea. Sadly, David was killed in the battle of Osan on July 5, 1950. Belinda and David named their beautiful daughter Harlem after the borough, Harlem, in Bronx, New York where they met. Harlem never knew her father. All she had was a picture of the three of them on her dresser. Harlem would kiss the picture every night before she went to bed and every morning before she got out of bed.

"Harlem, I hope you didn't brush your teeth yet. You're just going to have to brush them again after you eat. How many times have I told you that?" Belinda said from the kitchen.

"I know Mama. I've got to go back that way anyway. I forgot to say good morning to Daddy."

After breakfast Harlem hurriedly brushed her teeth again then ran back into her room. She couldn't leave without talking to her daddy.

Harlem picked up the picture she had on her dresser and said, "morning Daddy, first day of school. I'll let you know how everything went when I come home. Just hope I don't get Sister Delores for my teacher. Pray for me that I don't."

There was a knock at Belinda's door.

"Now who in the world is that this early in the morning?" Belinda said in a puzzling voice to herself.

Belinda opens the door. It's Mrs. Doris Archer, Belinda's good friend and neighbor and Harlem's babysitter.

Mrs. Archer said, "Belinda, hate to bother you, but do you have any extra milk. I forgot to pick it up at the store yesterday and Leon doesn't have any for his cereal. You know how that is. You don't want to send your baby to school on an empty stomach."

"Sure, come on in, I'll get you some milk," Belinda said.

Doris asked Belinda in a puzzling voice, "you sending Harlem back to St. Anthony's again this year. Ain't that costing you quite a bit when she can go right up the road to Bronx Elementary for free? Don't Harlem feel funny in a school with all white folk anyway?"

"Doris! What an awful thing to ask!" Belinda said surprised at the question.

"Well, it's the truth. Why can't she go to school with her own kind?" Doris adamantly asked Belinda.

"What do you mean Doris, her own kind? You forget Doris, the man I loved and married - her father was white. Her skin is a little browner than the rest of the kids and no she doesn't feel funny. Harlem has a lot of friends there, white and colored. Doris, I mean no disrespect, but St. Anthony's is a good school and it is run by some strict nuns that don't take any nonsense off of a bunch of insolent children. There is no playing around and no rudeness is tolerated. And as far as paying St. Anthony's, they give me a big break, because I do all the washing and ironing of the linens used on the altar at mass and any other task they give to me to do. It's all about Harlem getting the best education that I can give her. Doris, this is what I want for Harlem."

"Ok, ok. Sorry I said anything. It just sounds to me like you're working yourself too death, but that ain't none of my business," Mrs. Archer said.

Doris turns to go out the door and looks back at Belinda. "Thanks for the milk. Sorry for questioning your reasons for sending Harlem to another school Belinda. Sometimes I don't know when to keep my mouth shut. I guess I wish I had your determination to make life better for Leon. Guess I'll see Harlem tonight after school then."

"Sure. I'll drop Harlem off right after school, and then I'll pick her up tonight around 9:30 after my last nursing class. And Doris, don't worry about what you said to me earlier. You have a right to ask me anything you want to. That's what friends do when they are concerned about each other."

"Belinda just be careful. Those streets are dangerous out there, especially at night with those gangs," Doris said in a concerned voice.

"Don't worry Doris. I know how to take care of myself."

Doris hollers to Harlem, "see you tonight Harlem. Have a good day at school."

"Thanks Mrs. Archer. See you tonight," Harlem hollered back.

Harlem ran out of the kitchen with a hair brush in her hand. "Mama, can you put my hair in two pigtails and put these two ribbons around them?"

"Ok Harlem, hurry or we are going to be late. Harlem did I ever tell you how proud I am of you?"

"You tell me all the time Mama. Mama, tell me again how you met Daddy."

"Harlem, I've told you so many times."

"Yeah, but I love to hear that story Mama. I wish he was here now. I miss having Daddy with us."

Belinda brings Harlem closer and hugs her.

"Baby, I know you missed out on having a daddy like the rest of the kids, but he is always in our hearts and I told you I see him all the time in your pretty blue eyes."

"Just tell me Mama one more time about how you met Daddy."

"Ok, but it's the short version because we are going to be late young lady."

Belinda takes Harlem's hands and tells her the story for about the fiftieth time.

"Your daddy was on leave from the Army. He would take the ferry to Harlem, where I lived with my parents at the time, just to look at the sites. Well, I saw this tall, sandy-haired, handsome man come into the candy store where I was working one day in his impressive uniform. His eyes were so blue and bright, just like your eyes, and he had that crooked little smile that you have. I could feel this warmth radiating from his eyes and I felt I could look into his soul; the soul of a good man Harlem. We talked. He always told me that I looked a lot like Lena Horn, the singer. I didn't know if he was just trying to make small talk or out-right telling me a fib. I would just laugh when he would say that. He came back again about two more times and he finally asked me out. We fell head over heels in love with each other and got married. The end. Now let's go!"

Belinda gave Harlem her lunch box and book bag and out the door they went in a hurry so Harlem wouldn't be late for school and Belinda wouldn't be late at the clinic.

chapter 2

THE HEAT WAS unbearable that morning, especially for the first day of school. This was a typical early September day in New York. Fall was just around the corner and would be a grateful reprieve from the terrible hot summer that everyone endured that year.

Harlem was so excited that she didn't notice the heat or smells of the peanut vendor or Mr. Starksy's polish hotdogs he sold from the little stand across the street. Mr. Starksy was a big man with big shoulders and a big handlebar mustache. Harlem thought he looked a little scary.

Harlem looked forward to seeing her old friends, especially Arlene Dabrowski and Joseph MacKenna. Arlene and Joseph were from Woodlawn which is in North Bronx. They would be riding the bus to school. There was no bus transportation for Harlem. Anyone from South Bronx had to walk to St. Anthony's Catholic School.

A few blocks up the street Mr. Abermann, an older Jewish gentleman in his late eighty's, who owns a small grocery store on the block, stopped Belinda and Harlem to talk for a few minutes. "How pretty you look, little Harlem. You're as pretty as your mom. How would you like a nice shiny apple for your lunch today?"

Harlem looked up at her mother for approval to accept the apple.

Belinda looked at Mr. Abermann and said, "thank you Mr. Abermann." She then looked at Harlem and asked, "would you like this apple to eat with your lunch today Harlem?"

Harlem took the apple from Mr. Abermann's hands and noticed a number on his lower arm. "Thank you Mr. Abermann. How come you have this number on your arm? Is it your address or phone number?"

Mr. Abermann looked down at Harlem with somewhat of a sad look in his eyes and said, "no little one. A long time ago in a faraway country some bad people put that number on my arm."

Harlem looking puzzled, asked Mr. Abermann another question. "Why would somebody do that to you Mr. Abermann, you're such a nice man?"

Belinda takes Harlem's hand. "Sorry Mr. Abermann, she is full of curiosity. Harlem we have to go now. We'll talk about this one day when you can understand things a little better."

Harlem said, "but Mama . . ."

"There you go again with your "but Mama". Let's go."

Harlem looks up at Mr. Abermann. "Bye Mr. Abermann. Thanks for the apple."

Mr. Abermann looked at Harlem and said, "you have a nice day Harlem!"

Just then two street walkers that know Belinda from being treated at the clinic say hi to Belinda.

"Miss Belinda, Miss Belinda, its Lucy and Hazel."

Belinda turned around said, "hi girls. It is a beautiful day today."

Lucy answers Belinda. "Oh, it sure is Miss Belinda. Is that Harlem? She's so cute. Hazel, look at her pretty ribbons on her pigtails."

"Yes, this is my little girl. It is her first day of school. We have got to be on our way, no time to talk today girls," Belinda said.

Harlem looked up at her mother and said, "Mama, who are those ladies? They sure are dressed funny and they got that stuff smeared all over their faces. How did they know I was your little girl?"

"Well Harlem, they come into the clinic when they are hurt or sick and we treat them according to whatever their illness is that day. It just so happens I have a picture of you on my desk."

"What kind of sickness do they get Mama?"

"There are all kinds of sicknesses Harlem, bad colds, the flu. We treat them so they can go back to work."

"Where do they work Mama?"

"Harlem, I really don't know. I don't ask. We just try to make them better," Belinda said.

As they walked Harlem held her mother's hand tightly as they maneuvered from one side of the street to the other to intentionally stay away from the criminal activity that was prevalent on the street that morning. All Harlem could think about was who her new teacher would be, until her thought was interrupted by one of the white gang members calling out to them.

"Hey pretty mama. Ya' got a' pretty lil' zebra kid."

Harlem hollered back at the gang member. "I'm no zebra you crazy man."

Belinda said, "Harlem be quiet and just keep walking. What's wrong with you? I told you to ignore these people when we walk through here. It's dangerous to even look their way. Don't ever answer them again, do you understand me?"

"But Mama, he called me a zebra and he doesn't even know me."

Belinda firmly grabbed Harlem's hand and proceeded to walk even at a much faster pace. Belinda was unknowingly dragging Harlem down the street.

"Ouch, Mama, my hand, you're squeezing it too tight and I can't keep up with you, what's wrong?"

Belinda stopped suddenly, stooped down to Harlem's level, grabbed her shoulders and said in a stern voice that Harlem very seldom heard coming from her mother. "Harlem, these streets are full of bad people with sick minds from drugs or just plain mean and sick, I don't know. We walk these streets every day and you have to learn to stay as far away from them as you can and keep your mouth shut no matter what they say or they will hurt you Harlem. That man is in a gang and the gangs in this area are out to hurt people. You cannot make eye contact or even answer them. You just keep walking. Do you understand what I just said because it is important that you do?"

"But Mama, they . . ."

"No but's, you heard what I said and I know you understood what I said. There's no more to say. Now let's go or you're going to be late for school and I'm going to be late for work at the clinic."

Harlem knew her mother was mad and tried to change the subject.

"Mama, I hope I don't get Sister Delores for my teacher. She is so mean."

"Harlem, Sister Delores is not mean, she is just strict and doesn't want any foolishness going on in her class. You're there to learn not play so one day you can go to college and become a doctor like you told me that you wanted to be when you grew up. I want us to be able to get out of this city and live in a safer town so that you can go outside and play like a normal little girl should, and not be afraid. This is why I take nursing classes at night so that I can become a registered nurse and make more money than I'm getting now as an LPN. Do you understand what I just said?" Belinda said.

"Yes ma'am, I understand, but I still hope I don't get Sister Delores for my teacher."

Belinda just shook her head.

As they rounded the corner to St. Anthony's, the school buses started to enter and drop off the children.

Belinda looked down at Harlem. "Here we are Harlem. You look so pretty in your uniform."

"I think I look like a checker board."

They both laughed.

Even though Harlem was anxious to start school, Belinda knew she was somewhat nervous.

Belinda said, "Harlem, same rules as last year. I will be here to pick you up right after school. Do not – and I stress DO NOT leave the school until I get here. I'll walk you home and Mrs. Archer is going to watch you until I get home from school tonight."

"But Mama after you take me to Mrs. Archer's, you have to walk all the way back here to the hospital for your classes and I worry about you."

"Lordy girl, you're too young to worry. Leave the worrying up to me. It's only two nights a week, and sometimes the instructor lets us out a few minutes early. Now go see if your friends are here. I love you girlie. Now give me a hug. Love you baby girl."

Harlem hugs her mother.

"Love you to Mama, see you tonight."

Belinda walks off while Harlem is waving to her.

Just then Arlene's bus pulls up. Arlene got off the bus, but there is no Joseph.

Harlem runs up to Arlene.

"I'm so glad to see you Arlene. I missed you," Harlem said.

Arlene said, "I missed you too Harlem."

Harlem watched as the last child got off the bus.

"Where is Joseph, Arlene?"

With a sad and distant look in her eyes Arlene said, "Joseph won't be coming back to school for a while Harlem. He has a disease."

"What do you mean disease? What kind of disease?" Harlem asked.

"I don't understand, but the disease cripples your legs. My mother called it polio."

The bell rang and the conversation was cut short between the girls.

All Harlem could think about was her friend Joseph and this disease he has called polio.

"What in the world was it?" All Harlem could picture was how Joseph loved to play kickball and catchers. He couldn't play these games anymore with crippled legs.

Harlem said to herself, "Mama will know what polio is. She's smart and going to be an RN when she finishes her night classes."

Just then her world stopped when she heard her name called to stand in line with the other third graders.

"Harlem Rose O'Brannan, Harlem Rose, PAY ATTENTION AND GET IN LINE – NOW!!"

When Harlem looked up, she saw Sister Delores.

"Harlem Rose, if I have to call your name one more time, you get the ruler!" Sister Delores said.

Harlem knew what that meant – a crack across the knuckles.

"Sorry Sister Delores," Harlem said.

Sister Delores reminded Harlem of Mr. Starsky except she was a woman of color like Harlem's mother. She was very tall and had these broad shoulders like he did. Her voice was very deep and loud at times.

Harlem ran over and got in line. She tried to make herself feel better and remember what her mother said about Sister Delores. "She's not mean, she's not mean, she's not mean."

Next Sister Delores said, "Arlene Dabrowski. Arlene, get in line behind Harlem."

Harlem was so excited that Arlene was going to be in her class. She felt so much better. Maybe it wouldn't be so bad in Sister Delores's class since Arlene was in there with her.

"Harlem, I had the most wonderful summer. My mom, my dad and my brother and I took a trip to Maine. We went fishing and stayed in this really nice cabin in the woods. I learned how to swim and everything. What did you do?" Arlene asked.

Harlem replied, "well, my mom and I went . . ."

Just then the morning bell rang and Sister Delores bellowed out, "let's go class. Not a word, single file to Room 103 down the hall and to the left."

Harlem was glad this time the bell rang. All she could think of was should I lie and tell Arlene I had fun this summer like she did or should I tell the truth? The truth is, I stayed inside all summer and read books because it's too dangerous to be outside in the projects. After all, Arlene was her best friend even though she had to wait until school started to see her again. No, lying was out of the question. Harlem knew her mother taught her that lying gets you nowhere and that one lie leads into another lie.

Harlem got through the first day of third grade without having to answer Arlene's question about what she did all summer. Most of the children had their minds and attention on listening to Sister Delores and what she was teaching that day, and, of course, her strict rules that she listed on the blackboard that everyone MUST memorize.

The last bell for the day rang, and everyone filed out of St. Anthony's in an orderly manner to either get on their assigned buses or walk home.

Harlem stood outside while the children got on their buses and waved goodbye to Arlene as her bus left. Harlem then sat on the school steps to wait for her mother to pick her up from school for the long walk home.

chapter 3

As HARLEM SAT on the steps of St. Anthony's school and watched Arlene's school bus leave, she couldn't help but feel a little envious of Arlene and wonder what life would be like with both parents, and a real home in the suburbs away from the constant noise, fighting and gun shots fired day or night. But most of all, what would life be like not to be afraid all the time.

Harlem, unknowingly, started to think out loud, "God, if you can hear me, please take me and my mama away from here and find us a nice home like Arlene has and . . ."

"And what Harlem? Who in the world are you talking to?" Belinda asked as she started up the steps to St. Anthony's.

"Nobody Mama. I was just wondering out loud about the homework Sister Delores gave us for tomorrow's class."

"Well, so you got Sister Delores for your teacher. How did everything go today?" Belinda asked.

"I know Sister Delores is strict, but I remembered what you said this morning. I am here to learn, not play because I really, really, really want to be a doctor one day."

"Good for you Harlem. I'm glad you are starting to understand what I'm trying to get through to you. You wait right here. I have to go in and pick up the cloths on the tabernacle so I can wash them for mass on Sunday."

Belinda comes back out of St. Anthony's in a few minutes and tells Harlem, "let me get you home Harlem, it's been a long day for both of us."

As Belinda and Harlem are walking back to the projects, Belinda can sense that something is bothering Harlem.

Belinda asked, "Harlem, you look a little sad. Are you sure everything went ok in school today. I told you, you can tell me anything."

Harlem said, "well, there is something I don't understand. You remember Joseph McKenna?"

"Yes, isn't he Arlene's friend?" Belinda replied.

"Yeah, but Arlene said he won't be back to school for a long time because he has polio. Mama, what is polio?"

"Polio is a disease from the poliovirus. It causes people to become paralyzed. Paralyzed means you can't move your arms, legs, or you may not be able to breathe on your own."

Harlem said, "I know what paralyzed means. We had that word last year in the second grade. I just don't want to think that Joseph can't run or walk and play anymore."

Belinda said, "I know it hurts to think of your friend that way, but thankfully in 1952, a man named Jonas Salk discovered a cure for polio. I couldn't get you a shot for polio until 1955 when it was approved. Don't you remember? You didn't like getting that needle very much. Well, you got two separate doses of the vaccine to prevent you from getting polio."

"Why didn't Joseph's mom and dad get him a vaccine?" Harlem asked.

"It's very complicated Harlem. Maybe the virus was already in his system and it was too late for the doctors to help him. Look, I want you to stop worrying about Joseph. He probably got the vaccine by now and it will just be a matter of time before he starts to feel better." Belinda tried to reassure Harlem.

"I'll try not to worry Mama. But it is hard to think that he can't run and play anymore."

"I know, I know. Maybe one day you and I can take the bus and visit him."

Harlem sounding a lot happier said, "oh! I would really like that and maybe Arlene can be there when we go. Oh, look Mama, there's Mr. Abermann."

"How was school today Harlem?" Mr. Abermann asked.

"Great! Especially lunchtime and that apple was delicious that you gave me," Harlem exclaimed.

"I'm glad to know that you enjoyed it. Maybe there will be another one tomorrow morning," Mr. Abermann said.

"Mr. Abermann, you can't afford to be giving away apples every day," Belinda said.

"How often do you get to meet a nice, mannerly, smart little girl like Harlem in this part of town—NEVER. So If I have an extra apple here and there to give away, it goes to Harlem," Mr. Abermann said in an adamant voice.

Belinda laughed. "I won't argue with you Mr. Abermann, its hopeless!!"

"You just be careful. It is starting to get darker a little earlier now. You and Harlem take care Belinda."

"We will. See you tomorrow morning," Belinda said.

Belinda took Harlem right to Mrs. Archer's apartment.

"Mrs. Archer, I'll be back around 9:30 to pick up Harlem. Don't wake her if she is still asleep, I'll just carry her to our apartment."

"Belinda, please be careful. The streets are so bad at night," Mrs. Archer said.

"Mrs. Archer, you're going to scare Harlem. Don't worry about me. Give me a hug Harlem."

Harlem hugs Belinda.

"Hurry up and be a nurse Mama," Harlem said as she hugged her mother.

"You're too funny Harlem. I have one more year to go and there will be a lot of changes around here. Now go do your homework."

Harlem ran to the window and watched as her mother walked down the sidewalk until she was out of view.

chapter 4

IT WAS 8:45 p.m. and the nursing instructor let class out early at Bronx General Hospital.

"See you next Thursday night Belinda. Don't forget to study for the test," Linda said.

"Linda, don't even worry about that. I'll be reviewing my notes in my sleep tonight."

"Belinda, are you sure I can't give you a ride home?"

"Thank you Linda, but it is out of your way, and in the city in all that traffic. It's really not that far. See you Thursday."

The night air was a little cooler compared to the early morning heat that September morning. Belinda could tell autumn was in the air. Belinda even noticed as she walked how unusually quiet the streets were. All Belinda could think of was, "one more year, and Harlem and I can move at least into a half way decent apartment building until I can afford a home."

Belinda was almost in front of Mr. Abermann's store when she heard gun shots. She started running to Mr. Abermann's store hoping if she hollered and pounded on the door he would come down from the upstairs apartment and let her in.

Belinda made it to Mr. Abermann's front door and hollered and beat on the door for him. He turned the light on and started to come down the steps.

Two more shots were fired and Belinda's voice was silent. The pounding stopped.

Mr. Abermann opened his door and saw Belinda lying on the sidewalk. She had been shot in the back of the head, but was still alive.

Mary Wagner

While cradling Belinda in his arms, Mr. Abermann cried out, "help, somebody help, call an ambulance. Belinda, Belinda stay with me, stay with me!!"

It seemed to Mr. Abermann that it took an extra-long time before an ambulance arrived. Just then the ambulance arrived with the police.

While the ambulance attendants were working on Belinda, the police talked to Mr. Abermann.

"Sir, my name is Sergeant William Albrecht and this is Officer Manny Lopez of the Bronx Police Department, Precinct 12. Sir, can you tell me what happened?"

"What took you people so long? I know, I know it's got to be this part of town. Doesn't matter who dies here. The more people get shot, the less you guys have to come here. I'm an old wise Jewish man, not a stupid old man!!"

"Don't need the harassment. The call came in and we got here as fast as we could," Sergeant Albrecht said.

While Sergeant Albrecht questioned Mr. Abermann, Officer Lopez took notes.

"Sir, what is your full name, what happened, and how do you know this lady?" Sergeant Albrecht asked.

"My name, Sergeant Albrecht, is Telly Abermann. I heard gunshots. That sir is not unusual around here but you probably already know that. I heard someone shouting my name and pounding on the door. I recognized the voice as a lady in the neighborhood that frequents my store with her daughter at least twice a week. I heard two more shots. I opened the door and saw Belinda with blood pouring from the back of her heard lying at my stoop. I hollered for someone to call the ambulance and held her until you got here. The lady's name is Belinda. I don't know her last name. If this old body could have gotten down the steps a little faster maybe she wouldn't have been shot."

"There was probably nothing you could have done to prevent this Mr. Abermann. A colored woman out on this street this time of night. You don't know what she was involved in," Sergeant Albrecht said.

Mr. Abermann's eyes grew bigger with a look of disgust at the sergeant and said, "I'm going to ignore what you just said about a lady you don't even know. Belinda is one of the smartest, honest, nicest, and above all a genuine great lady. She was coming from Bronx General

16

where she is studying for her RN license. You assumed because she was colored that she was involved in some kind of crime. You should be ashamed!"

Sergeant Albrecht looked down on Mr. Abermann with a sneer on his face and said, "look old man, I don't care if she's a nun, or discovered electricity, she's colored and between me and you she's up to no good being out in this neighborhood this time of night. I personally don't care what you think or how you feel."

Mr. Abermann, shocked, looked at Sergeant Albrecht and Officer Lopez and said, "I'll report you tomorrow morning for what you just said to me. I'm not afraid of you. You see these numbers on my arm. I was in a concentration camp in Poland for three years. You don't scare me."

Sergeant Albrecht looked at Mr. Abermann with that smug smile of his and said, "you do that. Who's your witness old man? Officer Lopez didn't hear a thing. You better watch your back Telly or you're going to wish you were back in a concentration camp in Poland."

Sergeant Albrecht was a forty- five year old white man of German descent, tall and thin, with deep acne marks on his face. What hair he had was somewhat blonde. He was also a cigarette chain smoker and carried that cigarette odor not only on his body, but also in the squad car.

Officer Lopez was quite the opposite of Sergeant Albrecht. He was in his thirties, a little shorter, muscular, tanned, with dark hair and very handsome. He didn't smoke and couldn't stand to sit in the squad car with the stench of cigarettes everywhere.

When the ambulance left with Belinda to go to Bronx General, Sergeant Albrecht summoned for Officer Lopez to get back in the squad car and tauntingly said to Mr. Abermann, "don't you worry about a thing Mr. Abermann. We'll question the folks at the hospital and get this colored lady's last name and find out where she lives. Take care now. Oh yeah, we'll probably, if we have time, question people in the neighborhood about the shooting. Let's go Lopez, we're through here."

Officer Lopez turned to Sergeant Albrecht and said, "go get in the car Serge, I have a few things to clear up in my notes with Mr. Abermann."

Sergeant Albrecht shouted out," two minutes Lopez, two minutes and we're out of here."

Officer Lopez hesitated and looked at Mr. Abermann and said, "I'm sorry for Sergeant Albrecht's rudeness. I, myself, will do everything I can to find the person or persons who did this to your friend."

Mr. Abermann looked up into Officer Lopez's eyes and said. "I see goodness and fairness in your eyes. I trust you. But Officer Lopez, watch this man you work with all day. I see evil in his eyes."

As the police drove off, Mr. Abermann raised his fist to the air and said, "God, if you can bring the plague of the locust back, let them consume that car, and turn it into dust and send it to hades, but spare Officer Lopez!!"

chapter 5

MRS. ARCHER PACED back and forth. It was going on 11 o'clock at night. Where was Belinda? She had no way of making a phone call and had no idea what building Belinda had her classes in. All she could do was stare out the window then look at Harlem asleep on the couch. She knew that Belinda was a person of her word and if she said she would be home by 9:30, she would be home.

"I know something happened, I just feel it," Mrs. Archer said as she talked quietly to herself.

Just then she heard a clamber in the hallway outside of her door.

"My gracious what in the world is going on out there?"

The noise woke Harlem up and while rubbing the sleep from her eyes looks up puzzled at Mrs. Archer.

"Mrs. Archer, is Mama home yet? What's all that noise in the hallway?"

Mrs. Archer peered through her peep-hole in the door and noticed two policemen banging on Belinda's door.

"I knew it, I knew it, Oh my Lord, I just knew it!" Mrs. Archer said with a shaking voice.

"You knew what Mrs. Archer? Is something wrong?" Harlem asked.

"Harlem, I am going out in the hallway. You stay here until I come back, don't come out here, understand?"

"Yes ma'am, but hurry back," Harlem said in a frightened voice.

Just then Leon comes out of the bedroom to see what all the raucous is about.

Mary Wagner

Mrs. Archer shouted to Leon, "Leon, get back in bed and close the door and stay in there."

Trembling, Mrs. Archer shuts the door behind her and walks over to the two policemen.

These two policemen were the same two that were at the crime scene where Belinda was shot.

Mrs. Archer, with her voice quivering said, "can I help you sir?"

"As a matter of fact lady you can," Sergeant Albrecht said, without even introducing himself or Officer Lopez.

"We were told a Belinda O'Brannan lived here with her daughter. Is that correct?" Sergeant Albrecht said.

"Yes sir, yes sir, she does and I'm babysitting her daughter until she comes home from school. Is everything alright?" Mrs. Archer said, with her voice still trembling.

In an almost callous tone in his voice, Sergeant Albrecht said, "well no, she won't be coming home tonight or any other night. She was shot around 9 o'clock tonight. She was taken to Bronx General and died about an hour ago."

Mrs. Archer slumps to the floor in disbelief. Crying, she tells Sergeant Albrecht, "her little girl, Harlem, is in my apartment. I have to be the one to tell her, not a stranger!"

Sergeant Albrecht looked at Officer Lopez and said, "help her up Lopez. I'll go in and tell the girl about her mother."

Mrs. Archer couldn't get over how insensitive this policeman was and knew she had to be the one to tell Harlem about her mother.

Mrs. Archer got up, stood in front of the door and said to Sergeant Albrecht, "I want to let Harlem know about her mother, please!"

Officer Lopez looked at Sergeant Albrecht and said, "Serge, it's what's best for the little girl. It's going to be a shock as it is. Let Mrs. Archer tell her about her mother."

"Ok lady, but make it quick. We have to take the girl to the precinct. Child Services is going to find her a place to stay until somebody from her family can take her," Sergeant Albrecht said.

Mrs. Archer looked puzzled at Sergeant Albrecht and said, "what do you mean, take her to the precinct? Why can't she stay here tonight?"

"Are you related to her lady or do you have a license to care for foster children? If not, this is no concern of yours. Let's get this over with!" Sergeant Albrecht said with a harsh tone in his voice.

The three of them entered Mrs. Archer's apartment.

Harlem could tell something was wrong when she looked into Mrs. Archer's face.

With tears starting to form in Harlem's eyes she asked Mrs. Archer, "where is my mother? Did something happen to her? She didn't get hit crossing the street, did she Mrs. Archer? I want my mama. Is she in the hospital, I want to see her."

Mrs. Archer held Harlem close to her and said, "Harlem, your mama went to Heaven tonight. She's up there with your daddy."

Harlem started to scream, "No, no, I want her back, I want her back. It's my fault, my fault."

Mrs. Archer took Harlem's face into her hands and said, "Harlem, don't even go there. God wanted your mother tonight and he came for her. A very bad person hurt her. You didn't do anything but love her."

"No you don't understand. While I was waiting for her to pick me up today, I prayed to God to take us away from here. I killed her. It was me."

Officer Lopez stepped in front of Mrs. Archer, bent over to talk to Harlem and said, "I didn't know your mama and I don't know you very well Harlem, but you did nothing to cause your mother to be taken away from you. I see the love you have for her. A very bad person did this to your mother and it is up to the police to find this person."

Sergeant Albrecht looked at Officer Lopez and said, "Officer Lopez, can I talk to you for a few minutes in the hallway?"

"Sure, let's go," Officer Lopez said.

"I didn't know your middle name was "Dear Abby"," Sergeant Albrecht said while taunting Officer Lopez.

"What are you talking about? This is an eight year old girl who just lost her mother and we're taking her away to some strange place tonight. Put yourself in her shoes," Officer Lopez said with a sharp tone in his voice.

Sergeant Albrecht got into Officer Lopez's face and said, "that's your problem. A good police officer doesn't put himself in somebody else's shoes. Did you forget where you are tonight Lopez? There's a murder every other night on these streets. This is the projects Lopez. Nothing good happens here, nothing. This is all these people know."

Officer Lopez shook his head and said, "did you forget that I'm Puerto Rican, Serge. You think I don't know how you feel about me and the rest of the guys that don't have a last name that sounds like yours? And you're one hundred percent wrong about a lot of families that live in the projects. This little girl and her mother are good people, honest hard-working people, trying to dig their way out of the projects just like my family did. I feel sorry for you. You have a big red STOP sign in your brain on a Dead End street when it comes to people that aren't your color. Did the doctor cut your heart out when you were born?"

Sergeant Albrecht gives Officer Lopez a hateful grin and says, "tell you what. As of tomorrow morning you're getting written up for insubordination. Sleep on that tonight."

Officer Lopez stared right back at Sergeant Albrecht and said, "that's fine with me Serge. I forgot to tell you, that test I took a few months back, the one for detective. Well I was accepted. Until the class starts, I put my papers in for a transfer a few weeks ago for another unit in the precinct and a new partner. So you do what you got to do. I'm sure the captain would love to hear from Mr. Abermann and now Mrs. Archer. And by the way, I'm sure I'll sleep like a baby tonight, how about you?"

Officer Lopez turns and walks back into the apartment to try to console Harlem.

Mrs. Archer is holding Harlem and trying to comfort her.

"Harlem, you have to go with these policemen tonight. They won't allow you to stay here because I'm not part of your family," Mrs. Archer said.

"No, no, please don't let them take me, please Mrs. Archer, please," Harlem said while crying and holding onto Mrs. Archer.

Mrs. Archer looked at Officer Lopez and said, "can Harlem please go to her apartment and pack a few things? Maybe it will help her to have some of her things with her."

"Sure," Officer Lopez said. "I'm sure Sergeant Albrecht won't mind."

Mrs. Archer helps Harlem gather up her belongings, especially the picture on her dresser that she kisses every morning; the picture of her parents and her when she was a baby.

Mrs. Archer bends over and kisses Harlem and says, "Harlem, I'm going to come to see you as often as I can. I'll tell Mr. Abermann so he can come to see you too."

Mrs. Archer takes Harlem back to her apartment. Officer Lopez takes Harlem by the hand, carries her bag of clothes and belongings and puts her in the squad car.

Harlem, tears streaming down her face and crying uncontrollably, waves good-bye to Mrs. Archer as the squad car leaves the projects. Harlem knew her mother always wanted the two of them to be able to leave the projects one day, but it wasn't supposed to happen this way. The day that Harlem and her mother would leave the projects was supposed to be a happy day not a sad day.

chapter 6

After Harlem was taken to the police precinct, Officer Lopez took her into a small room with a few tables and chairs, soda and candy machines.

Officer Lopez stooped down and asked Harlem, "hey, how about a coke and a bag of chips until we can send out for some decent food?"

Harlem wouldn't speak. She just turned her head to the other side.

"Look Harlem, I can't imagine what you're feeling or what's going through your mind, but I'm not going to leave you until I find out where you will be staying," Officer Lopez said.

Still not speaking to Officer Lopez, Harlem hangs her head and stares at the floor.

Officer Lopez tries to communicate with Harlem again. "Listen, I lost my father to alcohol when I was six. My mother ran off when I was ten years old with some guy she met at a bar. If it wasn't for a special nun at St. Anthony's looking out for me, I probably wouldn't be here today either."

Harlem finally looks up at Officer Lopez with a surprised look and says, "did you really go to St. Anthony's because that's where I go to school?"

"I most certainly did. Small world isn't it Harlem," Officer Lopez said.

"Do you know Sister Delores? She is my teacher. She's kind of mean, but Mama said she is just strict so kids can learn more."

Officer Lopez gives Harlem a big smile and says, "Sister Delores was that special nun I told you about that looked out for me when my mother left me. Your mother is right Harlem. Sister Delores only tries to bring out the best in her students. I have to go down the hall for a few minutes and I'll be right back. Don't go anywhere."

In the meantime, Sergeant Albrecht is in Captain Randall's office making arrangements for Harlem to go to a group home until her next-of-kin can be found.

"Captain, I can have somebody come from that colored group home on the East side of town and pick the kid up tonight," Sergeant Albrecht said.

Captain Randall looks at Sergeant Albrecht and questions his advice. "I don't know Albrecht. That home is more for troubled teens, not an eight year old little girl. Plus she is light skinned with blue eyes. And with a last name like O'Brannan, how long do you think she'll last there?"

"Look Captain, she's no better than any other troubled kid that comes in here from the streets. We can't coddle these kids because they don't appreciate anything anybody does for them," Sergeant Albrecht said in his nasty, normal tone of voice.

Officer Lopez heard some of what Sergeant Albrecht said as he was coming into the room and said, "you're dead wrong Sergeant Albrecht. She's not a troubled kid and doesn't belong with troubled kids. I found a group home for Harlem. One where she will be taken care of until her next-of-kin is found. As a matter of fact, the person in charge will be here any minute."

"What group home is this Officer Lopez?" Captain Randall asked.

"It's the same group home I stayed in when I needed help – St. Anthony's."

Sergeant Albrecht snickered a little and said, "St. Anthony's doesn't have a group home. Whose leg you trying to pull Lopez?"

Captain Randall looks at Officer Lopez. "Lopez, is it true?"

"Captain," said Officer Lopez, "it is true they are not a group home, but they are qualified and have the paperwork that shows they can legally keep a child in their residence until that child can be placed with a relative. I should know. These sisters kept me until a family was found, a family according to their standards, and I thank God every day for the foster parents they picked for me."

"Captain, I hope you're not falling for this bologna," Sergeant Albrecht said.

"Look, it's getting late and as long as these nuns show me legal paperwork, the girl is in their care," Captain Randall said.

Sergeant Albrecht steams out of the office and gives Officer Lopez a dirty look and said, "you can't be leaving soon enough for me!"

Officer Lopez answers back, "two weeks can't come fast enough for me."

There is a commotion in the lobby of the precinct that can be heard in the Captain Randall's office.

Captain Randall looked up at Officer Lopez and said, "who is that, what is going on out there, check it out Lopez."

"Captain, I don't have to check it out, the voice is familiar. It's Sister Delores," Officer Lopez said.

"Well you better go get her Lopez before. . . "

"Before what Captain Randall? Why didn't you leave Harlem with Mrs. Archer? That would have been the safe and right thing to do. Instead you drag the little girl away from her familiar surroundings, away from the very people that can comfort through her grief. What's wrong with you people?" Sister Delores asked.

"There's nothing wrong with what we did. We went by the law. Mrs. Archer was not an authorized foster parent. We went by the book Sister Delores whether you like it or not," Captain Randall said.

"Well, I don't like it. And I bet that tender hearted Sergeant Albrecht was looking out for Harlem's best interest. I've heard all about how he treats the people in the borough. And if it were up to me, he'd be out of here. Captain, she is an innocent child," Sister Delores said in a displeased tone of voice.

"Do you know how many innocent children, seven and eight, are out on those streets and commit crimes?" Captain Randall said.

Sister Delores getting a little louder said, "arrest the parents, then take the child away from the environment and place him or her with decent law-biding citizens. And if you can't find any, come to St. Anthony's and ask for our help. Here are my legal papers, let me stress, LEGAL papers that enable me to take Harlem out of this place. Now take me to Harlem."

"Officer Lopez, take Sister Delores to Harlem. Log the girl out of the system. Nice to meet you Sister Delores," Captain Randall said in a smug voice.

Meanwhile, Harlem sat alone, staring at the floor, eyes swelled from crying, and still in shock over her mother's untimely death. Her head suddenly comes up and eyes are drifting towards the door upon hearing a familiar voice, a voice that is usually loud, but now is much quieter.

"Harlem, Harlem, its Sister Delores. You're coming back to St. Anthony's with me. Is that ok with you?"

"Sister Delores my mother is . . ." Harlem said with tears streaming down her face.

Sister Delores sits next to Harlem and hugs her.

"I know, I know Harlem. You're coming with me until a family member is found that you can stay with. That is if you want to," Sister Delores said.

"But there is nobody else. Mama never told me about anybody else. It was always just me and Mama," Harlem said.

"So you will stay with us at St. Anthony's as long as you want to. You'll be part of our family. Now let's get out of here. You need to be in bed, it's late. And you can skip school for a few days. I'm not as mean as you thought I was, am I Harlem?" Sister Delores said.

Harlem didn't say a word. She knew she did tell her mother that Sister Delores was mean. She never saw this tender side of Sister Delores before. She kind of liked it. She needed this kindness from Sister Delores at this time.

Harlem looked up at Sister Delores and said, "I'm ready to go home with you."

Sister Delores took Harlem's hand and Officer Lopez rode them home to St. Anthony's.

chapter 7

ST. ANTHONY'S CONVENT was almost a century old. The convent was the original church for years until the new St. Anthony's church and school was built some thirty years ago. There were some pretty big rooms constructed to accommodate the sisters in the old convent. The rectory for the priest's residence used to be part of the convent. Since St. Anthony's only had a visiting priest on Sunday's and Holy Days, it was not necessary to keep the rectory; hence, it became part of the convent years ago.

The convent housed eight sisters and three novices (sisters in training). The sisters shared bedrooms, two in each bedroom, except for Sister Delores who was in charge and had her own bedroom. The three novices shared one very large bedroom. Sister Delores had a small cot and a small three-drawer dresser put into the novices' bedroom for Harlem.

The first couple of days at the convent, Harlem was still grieving deeply over her mother's death. She kept to herself, didn't speak much and ate very little. Harlem didn't want to go to class. She didn't want to face her classmates. She didn't want to be questioned by the other kids or talk about what happened to her mother. Believe it or not, Sister Delores understood this and had to think of a plan to bring her out of this.

Sister Delores asked the only person she knew that could help Harlem, and that was Jesus. She could be found kneeling before the crucifix of Jesus many times asking him to please bring Harlem out of this depression.

Sister Delores made the sign of the cross before the crucifix and prayed. "Jesus, please show me the way. Show me how to help this little girl smile again, play again, be the Harlem that I have grown to know and care about through the years. The path that she and her mother have walked has not been an easy one. If there is someone out there that is a relative, please let them have the understanding and open mind to give Harlem the kindness and love she deserves. If she has no relatives, let the sisters of St. Anthony's be her new family. Thank you. Jesus, Mary, Joseph, pray for us." She makes the sign of the cross and rises from the kneeler.

Just then Father Dominic, one of the visiting priests, happened to overhear Sister Delores' prayer.

"Hope I'm not being intrusive Sister Delores, but I couldn't help but hear your prayer for that little girl whose mother was murdered," Father Dominic said.

"That's fine Father Dominic. Maybe the good Lord sent you in here to give me a suggestion on how I can help Harlem."

"Sister Delores, does Harlem have any close friends from her neighborhood or here at school that she could talk to?"

"Father Dominic, her mother never allowed her out of the apartment to play because of the violence in the streets, and the only friends I see her talk to are really during school hours. Thinking about it, there are two schoolmates whom she does share a lot of her time with, especially on the playground. Their names are Arlene Dabrowski and Joesph McKenna. Joseph didn't come back to school this year. Sadly, he contracted polio."

"There you go, Sister Delores. Why can't you talk to Arlene's parents, explain to them Harlem's situation, and get their permission to let her spend a weekend here with Harlem. That is, if you don't mind putting up with two little girls giggling and running around the convent and playground here at St. Anthony's. It won't be the 'fix-all' for Harlem, but it will take her mind off of this terrible trauma she is going through."

"Father Dominic, thank you. That might be just what she needs now. I'm going to call her parents tonight. Hopefully they will allow Arlene to stay the weekend."

"Sister Delores, how could they say no? What in the world can go wrong here? Do the police have any idea who did this horrible thing to her mother?"

"From my communication with the police department, I understand that Mrs. O'Brannan, Harlem's mother, was in the wrong place at the wrong time. I have been talking to Officer Lopez and he informed me that the department feels it was a gang shooting. Sadly, she was in the crossfire between two gangs. The police are hoping to find a snitch that will give up some information, but Officer Lopez said not to count on that. He said a snitch knows what will happen to him if the other gang members find out he talked to the police."

"I'm afraid Officer Lopez is right. It may take months or even years to solve this case. It is a very sorrowful situation for Harlem," Father Dominic said.

Father Dominic starts to walk away from Sister Delores but turns around and asks. "Have you had any luck in finding Harlem's next-of-kin or a distant relative by any chance? I'm not trying to put a damper on this situation, but you do know Harlem can't live here continually. The archdiocese will be expecting you to find her a foster family until a relative can be found."

"The Bureau of Missing Persons is working with our police department and Officer Lopez. I do know that sooner or later she will have go to a foster home if a relative can't be found Father Dominic. Being such a young child and having her mother taken away in such a horrible way, it is going to take several months for her to heal much less be taken away by a strange family she doesn't even know, then to be uprooted again to be with a blood relative if one is found."

"Sister Delores, is it you that needs to heal or is it Harlem? Think about it. You have been in this position before where you have had to find foster parents for a child. I feel this time something is different. I'll see you Sunday, and hopefully I'll see two happy little girls sitting in the pew on Sunday morning."

That evening Sister Delores called Arlene's parents and explained the situation to them about Harlem. They were delighted to have Arlene spend the weekend with Harlem.

The next Friday morning Arlene's parents brought her to school with her small suitcase to spend the weekend with Harlem. Harlem was so excited that she actually had this big grin on her face the whole day at school. Sister Delores had to put her teacher's face on and remind Harlem that it was a school day and try to refrain from talking and laughing so much with Arlene until after school. But Sister Delores had to admit to herself that she felt a burden of sadness lifted from her shoulders when she did see Harlem laugh and smile.

There was a moment on the playground when Arlene did talk to Harlem about her mother.

"Harlem, I'm sorry about your mother. If that happened to my mother, I couldn't be as brave as you are. You can come and visit me and stay at my house whenever you want and be part of my family."

Harlem, with tears in her eyes hugs Arlene and says, "Thank you Arlene for being my friend. Right now I have a family, a big family with the sisters here."

"Yeah, but I've got a dog and he is so cute. His name is Laddy. I can't wait for you to see him. Do you think Sister Delores would allow you to have a dog here?" Arlene asks.

"I don't know. What if Father Dominic is having mass on Sunday and the dog runs in? I'll be in a lot of trouble then. I think I'll wait a while before I ask Sister Delores about getting a dog. Come on, let's go down the slide some more. Tomorrow is Monday and I won't see you for a while. So let's play all we can today!!"

The weekend ended. But there were several more weekends that Arlene spent with Harlem.

The months slowly started to go by and Sister Delores happily noticed that Harlem was starting to get back to her old self again. Although there were several times Harlem was seen crying by the other sisters.

Someone once told Sister Delores that grief was a sorrow and sadness that slowly scatters, very slowly, through time until that person you have lost is a beautiful memory in your heart and mind that you never let go of or forget until God calls you home. She hoped that one day Harlem would reach that level and her mother would become that beautiful memory in her heart. But she could tell this grief wasn't going anywhere for months or even years to come.

Halloween passed, Thanksgiving passed and Christmas was around the corner. Christmas was Harlem's favorite time of the year. Sister

Delores knew that Harlem's first Christmas without her mother would not be easy. So she decided to give her a few Christmas chores to do at the convent that she knew Harlem would enjoy.

"Harlem, how would you like to help set up the manger and nativity scene for the altar. After that the other sisters and I are going to make these beautiful wreaths to go under each of the fourteen Stations of the Cross and you can help make those too. That's a lot of work, think you can handle it?"

"Handle it, yes ma'am Sister Delores, I know I can," Harlem said with big smile on her face that Sister Delores hadn't seen for months.

"All the statues and everything you need for the manger is in the back room in the closet in the vestibule. Start hauling it out because it will probably take you until Christmas Eve to finish it. Come on, get going!"

Harlem ran off in a hurry to retrieve all the items needed for the nativity scene.

Later on that evening while everyone was in church decorating, there was a knock on the door. The church doors are usually never locked, but with the trouble that was happening in the neighborhood, Sister Delores gave everyone instructions to lock the doors after 6 o'clock in the evening.

One of the novices, Sister Jean, opened the door and there stood Mr. Abermann.

"Hello Sister, my name is Telly Abermann, I'm here to see Sister Delores."

"I'll go get Sister Delores for you Mr. Abermann."

"Thank you Sister."

Sister Delores knows Mr. Abermann from the little stories Harlem would tell her. She also knew from Officer Lopez that he was with Belinda the night she was murdered.

"Hello Sister Delores, I'm . . . "

"I know who you are. Harlem described you to a 'T'. You're Mr. Abermann. So nice to meet you. How can I help you?"

"Well, maybe I can help you help Harlem," Mr. Abermann said.

Sister Delores said, "I'm for anything that can help Harlem at this time."

"I need to run this past you, Sister Delores, for your approval, because I really need to know that it is the right thing to do."

Puzzled, Sister Delores asks, "what is it Mr. Abermann? Come and sit with me in the back pew and we can talk."

Mr. Abermann asked Sister Delores, "did Harlem ever ask where her mother was buried?"

"Yes she did, and I also inquired. I called the mortuary and was told that they buried her within a week of her death in Potter's field. Mrs. O'Brannan had no money and no insurance. There was nothing I could do about it. Harlem took that quite hard but I explained to her that her mother's spirit was in heaven with her father. Why do you ask?" Sister Delores said.

"I ask you, Sister Delores, because the people at the mortuary lied to you. My cousin, Maury, who takes care of keeping names of people buried in Potter's Field in order and cross-referenced to the burial plot number, told me that Belinda O'Brannan was cremated. She wasn't buried in Potter's Field. He told me this a month ago. The mortuary knew it and tried to hide it. So, I took this old Jewish body down to the mortuary and found Belinda's ashes in a box sitting on a shelf. I thought 'oy vey' I can't leave this good lady sit on this shelf in this dirty basement like she never existed, so when Maury turned his back, I took her."

"Mr. Abermann, that's stealing," Sister Delores said.

"No! The way that lady was treated like she was nothing by that Sergeant Albrecht and now the mortuary is a disgrace!! Mr. Abermann said in an irate tone of voice.

Mr. Abermann bends over and takes a box out of a shopping bag he brought with him and hands a small sealed black box to Sister Delores

"Mr. Abermann, is . . ."

"Yes, Sister Delores, it is Harlem's mother, Belinda. And I also would like you to give this little box to Harlem at Christmas. It belonged to my wife. We had no children and I want Harlem to have it."

"Well, well, thank you, but I can't give her these ashes yet. I'm going to have to wait until the right time to explain what happened before I give them to her," said Sister Delores.

"I understand that. Can I get a peek at her?" Mr. Abermann asked.

"Why don't you just follow me, Mr. Abermann, and say hi to her?"

"No, no, I might upset her. You tell her Merry Christmas for me when you give her my gift. Merry Christmas Sister Delores."

"Merry Christmas to you too Mr. Abermann. You're a good, kind and decent man. May God bless you ten times over."

"He already has Sister Delores. I'm eighty-eight years old, had a beautiful bride by my side until she died in the concentration camp at Auschwitz-Birkenau in Poland. I lived. I had to find the will to go on. I have had a good long life. I can only wish a long and happy life for Harlem. Shalom Sister Delores."

Sister Delores shut the door, put the box of ashes and the small gift Mr. Abermann had for Harlem back in the shopping bag and watched Harlem as she scurried around trying to put the nativity scene together. She said to herself, "maybe, just maybe Harlem, this Christmas will help take some of the sorrow you have in your heart out and replace it with a little joy."

Sadly, two days later Mr. Abermann passed away. Sister Delores knew about his passing but she didn't want to upset Harlem. She wanted to wait until the right time to tell her.

chapter 8

CHRISTMAS EVE FINALLY arrived, but not without the first snowstorm of the season.

Harlem was so proud of the nativity scene that she worked on for weeks. She felt like an artist must feel on opening night at a gallery, showing off his or her finest painting for an admiring audience. The only difference would be that her opening night would be Christmas Eve Midnight Mass.

Sister Delores could tell that Harlem's spirits were finally being joyfully lifted up from the disheartened state they were in since her mother's death. Sister Delores even felt an excitement this Christmas that she had not felt for years. She knew that Harlem brought an enthusiasm into the convent and into the lives of the sisters that had been gone for years. Yes, Sister Delores felt that this may be the finest Christmas that she has had since being at St. Anthony's. The sisters, through Harlem's insistence and guidance, even put up a real Christmas tree in the convent. Harlem picked the tree out and Officer Lopez was nice enough to bring it to the convent. The decorations were made by the sisters and Harlem, and they were beautiful as they hung on the tree.

Before midnight mass started, Harlem's last finishing touch to the manger was to bring the "baby Jesus" into church and lay him in the manger. You would have thought this was Harlem's baby the way she had wrapped the statue and how she gently put him in the manger.

Sister Delores had a Bible that she and the other sisters were going to give Harlem for her Christmas gift. The Salvation Army also dropped off a pair of boots, two sweaters, mittens, leggings and a warm bulky coat for winter already wrapped and under the tree for Harlem. Officer Lopez also bought Harlem a "Tiny Tears" doll and a few games for her to play when Arlene would visit. These gifts were wrapped and under the Christmas tree for Harlem to open in the morning.

Harlem also made gifts for all the sisters. She knitted crosses for each of the sisters to be used as book markers for their Bibles or daily prayer books. Each one was a different color. Sister Delores had the most unique cross. Her cross was special. It was all white with a red border around it and three small red roses that Harlem knitted separately and was added to the cross when she finished making it. They really were beautiful. She learned how to knit from Mrs. Archer.

The church was starting to fill up. Harlem sat in the front row with the sisters. She was so proud of the nativity scene on the side of the altar. Everyone would comment on how beautiful it was. The more comments Harlem got the higher up on the pew she sat. Sister Delores told her she was going to float to the top of the church if her head got any bigger.

Watching the people as they came into church, Harlem noticed the two ladies her mother introduced her to the morning they walked to school, Lucy and Hazel. They both waved to Harlem and she waved back. Mr. Starksy and his wife also came into church and said hi to Harlem. It made her feel good to know that people her mother knew were there that night. The only ones that were missing were Mrs. Archer, Officer Lopez and Mr. Abermann. If they were there, Harlem thought, that would make it a perfect Christmas Eve.

Sister Rachael leaned over toward Harlem and said, "do you know those two colorful ladies Harlem?"

"Yes ma'am. My Mama said they came in her clinic a few times because they were sick. They are real nice ladies."

Sister Rachael snickered a little and said, "I bet they are really nice Harlem."

Sister Delores leaned forward staring at Sister Rachael and said in a stern voice, "It is not for us to judge people Sister Rachael. If Harlem says they are nice ladies, then that's exactly what they are – nice ladies."

Harlem just looked up at both sisters then looked around for Officer Lopez. She didn't see him, but there were so many people there she thought he may be way in the back of the church.

The snow kept no one away. There was standing room only. The choir sang Christmas carols before mass. Father Dominic came out of the sacristy before mass and whispered to Sister Delores, "I need to talk to you right after mass so don't go back to the convent. I'll be in the sacristy."

Sister Delores just looked puzzled and said. "Ok Father, I'll come back right after mass."

Midnight mass was beautiful. The choir sang magnificently. Tears were brought to a lot of faces, especially when the "Ave Maria" was sung at the beginning of mass.

After mass Sister Delores leaned over and said to Harlem. "I want you to go back to the convent with the other sisters. It has been a long day for you and it is really late, so go to bed. Father Dominic wants to talk to me. You never know what will be under the tree in the morning. Merry Christmas Harlem."

"Merry Christmas to you to Sister Delores." Harlem hugs Sister Delores then says, "I love you Sister Delores."

Sister Delores was taken back and didn't quite know how to react. Usually she kept her feelings inside, but not this time. Hugging Harlem with tears in her eyes, she said, "Harlem, I love you even more. Now you better get going."

Sister Delores waited in the pew while Father Dominic shook hands and wished the parishioners a Merry Christmas as they left the church. He then summoned Sister Delores to follow him into the sacristy.

She had this feeling in the pit of her stomach that something was wrong and Father Dominic would be the bearer of some kind of sad news. The only thing that ran through her mind was that she was going to be transferred to another church because there was such a shortage of nuns that year. She loved Saint Anthony's so much that it would really hurt her to have to leave.

Father Dominic picked a letter off of a table in the sacristy. "Sister Delores, this is a letter from the archdiocese of New York- His Eminence, the Archbishop. The letter states that you will no longer provide a residence here at Saint Anthony's for said Harlem Rose O'Brannan or any other orphaned or troubled child. There is no money in the budget to care for these children anymore. You can read the letter later. Harlem must be removed the day after Christmas to a state run group home or private foster care until a relative can be found."

"But Father Dominic, I don't understand. Why does the archdiocese care? She is just a little girl. She is no problem or trouble for the sisters and me. She takes up very little space. It won't cost the archdiocese any money to support her. What little bit of money we take in from the poor boxes can pay for . . ."

"Look Sister Delores there is nothing I can do about it. She has to go the day after Christmas. I told you she would not be able to stay here. Saint Anthony's is not an orphanage or equipped to be a foster home. Don't look so surprised, you knew this day would come," Father Dominic said.

Sister Delores replied, "remember what you said to me the day you saw me praying. You wanted to know if I were the one that needed healing. Well you were right." Sister Delores' voice is angry. "Look at my skin, Father Dominic. It's the same color of Harlem's skin. My mother was a white prostitute and left me on a street corner when I was five. I never knew who my father was. I went from foster home to foster home. I was beat, abused and called names you probably never heard before until I was put in a Catholic orphanage. The nuns accepted me, took care of me and above all showed me kindness and love that I never experienced in my life before. It didn't matter to them what color my skin was. This is why I became a nun. Then, yes, you're right, I needed healing. Do you know when I started to heal? I started to heal the day Harlem came here to stay. I let flow from my mind and body all the hurt I had locked up inside of me all those years, because I knew what Harlem was going through. I knew I had to help her."

"I'm sorry about the life you led as a child Sister Delores, but Harlem still has to leave the day after Christmas. Here are a list of qualified homes she can go to close to St. Anthony's so she doesn't miss school. I'd advise you to look this list over and pick a family. She has to be told tomorrow. I'm sorry. Now please try to understand where I am coming from and . . . .Sister Delores, I'm talking to you. Where are you going?"

"Sorry Father Dominic, I don't want to talk to you anymore!" Sister Delores, aggravated at the uncaring attitude of Father Dominic abruptly walks out of the sacristy and back to the convent.

chapter 9

THAT NIGHT SISTER Delores broke the bad news to the other sisters. They were quite saddened about the whole situation. Sister Delores and the other sisters prayed together for God to please keep Harlem in the convent as long as possible, at least until a real relative could be found. The prayers lasted well until the early morning hours of Christmas. They all were so tired they could hardly make it to their beds.

Christmas morning came and it was very quiet in the convent. Sister Delores was the first one up and noticed that Harlem wasn't up yet. "What little girl wouldn't be up, excited, running around, waiting to tear into her presents?" she said to herself.

She went into the novice's bedroom and noticed that the sisters and Harlem were still sleeping. She went over to Harlem and whispered, "time to get up. It's Christmas morning Harlem."

Harlem just moaned, "I don't feel good Sister Delores."

Sister Delores felt Harlem's head and she was burning with a fever. She had red spots all over her face, her arms and legs – her whole body. It looked like she had the chickenpox and had them pretty bad.

Sister Delores hollered for the novices to get up and run some cold water in the bathtub for Harlem. The fever was causing her to go in and out of consciousness.

"Dear God, I know we prayed for a miracle so that Harlem wouldn't have to leave the day after Christmas, but we didn't want her sick like this," Sister Delores said as she hurriedly wrapped Harlem in a sheet and put her in a tub of cold water.

"Sister Jean, please go into the vestibule in the church and call Dr. Hanson and see if he could come over here and look at Harlem. I wish

Father Dominic would take the time to see that our phone is fixed. It's been a month. Now that we have an emergency, someone has to run over to the church and call. Sorry, Sister Jean. I am upset over this high fever Harlem has. Thank you."

"Don't worry about it Sister Delores. I am upset too. But I am sure Father Dominic has done his best to get our phone fixed," Sister Jean said.

Sarcastically, Sister Delores says, "yeah, I bet he has!"

Dr. Hanson came over about an hour later. He said that Harlem had chickenpox and a bad case of them. He didn't want her to be around anyone for at least fourteen days. Dr. Hanson also noticed that Sister Delores had a terrible cough. "Sister Delores, that cough doesn't sound very good. Why don't you come by the office tomorrow and let me give you a good check-up?"

"Dr. Hanson, right now my main consideration it getting Harlem well. I've had this cough for a few weeks. I think I am allergic to something. Promise, I'll be by as soon as Harlem is on her feet."

"It's up to you Sister Delores. Don't make a promise you can't keep. A simple cough can turn into something worse if you don't take care of it. I'll be by in a few days to check on Harlem. Now all of you ladies enjoy the rest of the day and have a Merry Christmas."

The sisters also wished Dr. Hanson a Merry Christmas as he went out the door.

The sisters were elated – not about Harlem being sick, but knowing she at least has another fourteen days with them. Sister Delores knew she had to act fast. She knew some of the families that were on the list for foster care that Father Dominic gave her and she did not approve of any of them.

Sister Delores knew she had to get ahold of Officer Lopez to see if he could help them in any way possible to keep Harlem out of a foster home. She called the precinct and left a message for Officer Lopez to please stop by the convent to see her and that it was an emergency.

In the meantime, Father Dominic was told of the news and, of course, he wasn't very happy. He had to make the phone call to the archdiocese to let them know that Harlem couldn't be sent anywhere for at least fourteen days or more.

Harlem was very sick and weak. Christmas Day left without Harlem opening up any of her presents. The sisters waited on her and took turns with cold compresses on her head until the fever broke.

Two days later there was a knock on the door. It was Officer Lopez. He apologized to Sister Delores for not coming right away but told her he went out of town to visit his foster parents. Of course she was very understanding and was just glad to see him. She told him of the dilemma that she was facing with the letter from the archdiocese instructing Saint Anthony's that they were not allowed to keep Harlem anymore. She was very vocal and adamant about not placing Harlem in a foster home.

"We only have twelve days Officer Lopez to find a relative that Harlem can live with. Have you heard anything at all about any relatives she may have?" said Sister Delores.

"The Bureau of Missing Persons contacted me this morning. From information we gathered from Mrs. Archer, Belinda's neighbor, Harlem's father was killed in the beginning of the Korean War. We know his name was David O'Brannan. They are going over the death records in Washington D.C. and hopefully will give us some information within the next couple of days. If we don't think we can meet the deadline, Sister Delores, I'm sure we can persuade Dr. Hanson to insist that Harlem needs extra time to recuperate," Officer Lopez said.

"So far the Good Lord has been with us. My only hope is that if there is a relative or relatives, that they accept Harlem, love her, be kind to her and are really good people. That's my wish for this little girl Officer Lopez. Her dream is to be a doctor one day. I would love to live long enough to see that dream come true."

"Sister Delores, believe me, you will be here and I'm sure Harlem will invite both of us to her graduation from medical school. And you don't have to call me Officer Lopez all the time. Why don't you call me Manny, you always did before? After all, we go way back, and if it wasn't for you, there's no telling where I would be today or if I would even be alive."

"Manny, I call you Officer Lopez because I feel you should be respected. I was so young when you came to Saint Anthony's, twenty years old to be exact. I think you were about ten. I was still a novice and hadn't taken my vows yet. Here we are together again. Manny, thank you for being such a good friend, especially at a time like this."

"If anyone should be thanked, it's you. Now let's go see how Harlem is doing," Officer Lopez said.

When they went into Harlem's bedroom, she was asleep. After two days of fighting a high fever, her little body was so weak and tired. Sister Delores woke Harlem up because she knew Officer Lopez couldn't stay too long and he wanted to see her for a few minutes.

"Harlem, Harlem, there's someone here to see you," Sister Delores whispered.

Harlem opened her eyes and was surprised. "Officer Lopez, did you have a nice Christmas? I'm so glad you're here!"

"I sure did. I heard you missed Christmas and didn't even get to open your gifts. How about I help you open a few gifts up. Yes, or no, it's up to you," Officer Lopez said.

"Yes, yes, yes. Is it ok Sister Delores?"

"Sure it is, as long as you feel up to it. You just sit up a little and Mann . . .Officer Lopez and I will give you a few of your gifts," Sister Delores said.

Harlem opened the gift of the Bible that the sisters gave her and was thrilled.

Officer Lopez helped her open up his gifts. She was so excited about the "Tiny Tears" doll and games. Harlem looked so much better. This was exactly the treatment for her illness that she needed.

The gifts from the Salvation Army were next. Harlem wanted to try everything on, but she was too weak to stand. Sister Delores told her winter was a very long time and she would have many days to wear her new boots, mittens and coat.

"The sisters and I want to thank you, Harlem, for our beautiful bookmarkers. You put a lot of hard work into making them. Every time I look at my bookmarker and see those tiny red roses, I'll think of you, Harlem Rose."

"Oh, I am so glad everybody liked their bookmarkers. It really wasn't that much hard work involved. I'm just glad you liked them," Harlem said.

The last gift to be opened was from Mr. Abermann, but Sister Delores held off on the gift he left for her. She knew how much Harlem liked Mr. Abermann and would probably ask a lot of questions as to why he didn't come to see her. She also wanted to explain the box with her mother's ashes in it. There was no sense in hiding what happened to her mother's body or waiting until Harlem got older. She needed to know and understand after she felt a lot better that the mortuary made a mistake even though Sister Delores knew they lied. It was no mistake.

"Well little lady I have to go back to work. I'll check with Sister Delores tomorrow to see how you're feeling." Officer Lopez gives Harlem a kiss on the cheek and says, "it's ok, I have had the chickenpox."

Sister Delores turned to Officer Lopez and said, "I'll walk you out Officer Lopez. You will probably have a busy night on the streets tonight."

Before Officer Lopez stepped out of the convent, he turned around to Sister Delores and said, "talking to the Bureau of Missing Persons is my first priority tomorrow. I don't want to see Harlem placed in a foster home either."

"Keep in touch Manny and thank you."

"I will. You're at the top of my list. Everything is going to be ok," Officer Lopez said.

chapter 10

FOURTEEN DAYS PLUS went by and Harlem, still weak and a few scars left from her chickenpox still showing on her face, started to feel so much better that she wanted to start back to school again. Sister Rita had been helping Harlem keep up with her school work while she was absent from school for the previous three weeks. Sister Delores told her she could start back to school as soon as Doctor Hanson released her to go back to school. Harlem missed her friends, especially Arlene.

Doctor Hanson insisted that Harlem was not to be placed in any foster home until she was released from his care, and he let it be known that he was in no hurry to release her. Of course Father Dominic wasn't too happy, but all of the sisters were overjoyed.

Sister Delores knew Harlem was feeling a lot better and that this would be a good time to explain to her about her mother's ashes and to give the Christmas gift to her from Mr. Abermann.

That evening while Harlem was doing her homework, Sister Delores interrupted her in order to have a conversation with her. "Harlem, can I talk to you for a few minutes? It won't take long. I know you have a lot of homework to do."

"That's ok, Sister Delores, I'm almost finished my homework anyway."

Sister Delores brought the two boxes out that Mr. Abermann gave her.

"Do you remember when you asked me to call the mortuary about your mother? I know we never talk about this but we have to now," Sister Delores said.

"Yes ma'am, you said my mama was buried in Potter's Field."

"Mr. Abermann stopped by the church one night. You were busy putting the nativity scene together and he didn't want to bother you," Sister Delores said.

Harlem replied, "I have been waiting to see him for so long. He should have talked to me."

"Well, he left you two boxes. One is a Christmas gift and the other I'll explain to you," Sister Delores said.

"That was so nice of him. He is a nice man. My mama always liked him so much!"

"Mr. Abermann knew someone at the mortuary and they told him that your mother wasn't buried in Potter's Field. The mortuary made a mistake."

"What does that mean a mistake?" Harlem asked.

"You know how we get ashes on our head on Ash Wednesday," Sister Delores asked.

"Yes, I remember "For dust you are, and to dust you shall return". But what does that have to do with my mother?" Harlem asked.

"Your mother was cremated Harlem. Her ashes are in this box."

"What's cremated mean?"

"It means your body is put in a special compartment, and what is left are your ashes."

Harlem started to cry. "My mother was burned. That's how you get ashes!"

Sister Delores said, "Harlem, I'll try to explain this the best way that I know how. Your mother felt nothing when she was cremated. Her body was a temporary home for her soul while on this earth until she died. Her soul went straight to Heaven to be with your father. On the last day, when God comes, her ashes, which are her body, will be reunited with her soul in Heaven. The mortuary made a mistake. You have your mother's remains with you now until you find the right time and the right place to bury her, yourself. Do you understand? This way when you find that special place to bury her, you will be able to place flowers on her grave and go there and even talk to her and let her know how everything is going in your life. Her spirit will always be with you. At least you know she's not in some big field where you will never be able to find her."

Harlem had tears in her eyes. She put her hands out and Sister Delores gave her the box of her mother's ashes. "I'll never let her go. She'll be with me always. I will find a place Sister Delores to bury her, but it really has to be a special place."

"Mr. Abermann also left you this little gift. He said it belonged to his wife and he wanted you to have it." Sister Delores hands the box to Harlem to open.

Harlem opened the box and her eyes got as big as marbles. "This is beautiful. It's a pin to wear on your dress. Look Sister Delores, it's beautiful!"

"It is so beautiful Harlem. I believe it is called a broach."

The broach was round with a large ruby in the center and eight large diamonds surrounding it. But there also was a note inside the box. The note read: *Harlem, I hope this broach brings you the happiness that it brought my wife. We managed to hide it from the Germans when they captured us that horrible night. They weren't meant to have the broach. Please keep the broach in a special place until you are older and wiser, because it may help you become the doctor that your heart yearns to become one day. Just remember me in your prayers. Not a day goes by that I don't ask God to look after you. Please don't be so sad Harlem. .That terrible sadness robs you of your beautiful spirit and the joy you so often bring to others. I know you will grow up to be a fine woman one day. Don't forget me. Your friend always, Mr. Abermann*

"What does he mean for me to keep it in a special place? Where would I put it?" Harlem asked.

"That's for you to decide," Sister Delores said.

Harlem opens up the lid to her mother's ashes and puts the box with the broach and letter inside the container. "Mama will look after this. It has to be the safest place right now. Can we go see Mr. Abermann so that I can thank him?"

"Harlem, Mr. Abermann passed away a few days after I talked to him. I didn't want to upset you before Christmas. Then Christmas day you were so sick that I thought it would be best to wait until you felt better before I let you know about his death. I don't think he wants you to be sad over his passing. He was a very generous man and all he wants in return from you is for you to remember him in your prayers.

With tears in her eyes Harlem looked up to Sister Delores and said, "I'll never forget him and I'll say a special prayer for him every night."

Sister Delores hugs Harlem. "Now you better get back to your homework and go to bed a little early tonight."

"Yes ma'am, I will. I love you Sister Delores."

"And I love you too Harlem. Good night."

"Goodnight."

chapter 11

SEVERAL MORE DAYS went by and January was almost over. Father Dominic was not very happy that Harlem was still staying with the sisters in the convent. He was the person who had to explain to the archdiocese why Harlem was still there. He was tired of the excuses coming from Sister Delores.

Father Dominic confronted Sister Delores after mass one Sunday. "Sister Delores, there will be no more excuses. You have until January 31st to choose a family on the list of foster parents that I gave you before Christmas. If you can't decide which family Harlem should go with, I will. As of February 1st, Harlem will be here no longer."

"I'm not giving you excuses. I am waiting to hear from Officer Lopez. I don't want to put Harlem in a home temporarily if a permanent home can be found with her own relatives. That to me would be cruel," Sister Delores said.

"No, what is cruel is my standing with the archdiocese. I have a chance to become Monsignor. But that's not going to happen if I keep giving the archdiocese excuses as to why she is still here. You know priests aren't the only ones that get transferred Sister Delores."

"Are you telling me Father Dominic that I will be transferred over this? If it means doing the wrong thing by putting Harlem in a foster home with a family I don't approve of, transfer me. You're not the holy man I thought you were. If you don't have a heart for a little girl and want what is best for her, then you should never be a Monsignor."

"I'm going to forget what you just said to me. But I am only going to warn you one more time. If you can't find a home for her by January

31st, I'll take the matter into my own hands on February 1st. Good-bye Sister Delores and have a nice day."

Sister Delores abruptly turned around. She couldn't believe that Father Dominic only thought of himself. She knew she had to get in touch with Officer Lopez right away. She waited until the church emptied out and Father Dominic was gone before she called from the vestibule.

Thankfully, Officer Lopez was on duty. She told him of the confrontation between her and Father Dominic and wanted to know if he had found out any information about Harlem's family.

"Yes, I was off yesterday and there was a message on my desk to call Washington. The message said that a relative of Harlem's was found. That's all I know. It's Sunday and the Department of Missing Persons is closed. I have to call tomorrow morning. Hopefully, it's good news. Just pray, Sister Delores, that this relative is a good person," Manny said.

"Manny, I've been praying for months. When you find out something, please stop by and let me know."

"I will. Please don't worry. I'll see you tomorrow," Officer Lopez said.

The next day Sister Delores was on pins and needles waiting for Officer Lopez to stop by. She tried to put her attention on her students that day, but anyone could tell her mind was elsewhere. She kept looking out the school window for Officer Lopez's squad car to pull up. She had feelings of happiness for Harlem, but the same time sadness would come over her. She had grown fond of Harlem and would really miss her if she left the convent. But she had to think of what was best for Harlem not her personal feelings.

It was lunchtime and the children were eating their lunches. Officer Lopez knocked on the door to the classroom and Sister Delores, looking through the window in the door, motioned for him to stay there. She went out into the hallway where she and Officer Lopez could talk in private.

"Harlem has a grandfather living in West Virginia Sister Delores. It seems he had no idea his son David married Harlem's mother. David kept his marriage a secret. Maybe he was hesitant to let them know his wife was colored and he didn't think they would accept her as his wife. I don't know what was in his mind. A telegram is being sent to the grandfather today to let him know he has a granddaughter and when she will be arriving in West Virginia. I hate to be the one to tell you, but Father Dominic already contacted the Child Welfare Services to make arrangements for Harlem to leave within the next couple of days," Manny said.

"That was no surprise to me that Father Dominic would want to hurry this situation. Manny, what is her grandfather's name? Where in West Virginia does he live? Does he have a home? What kind of man is he? What happened to his wife? What . . . ?"

"Hold on, I don't know a whole lot. His name is Brady O'Brannan. He lives in a small town in West Virginia called Kolter. He doesn't exactly live in the town. I was told he lives in the mountains. His wife died right after they got the news of their son's death. Her name was Kathleen Rose. Isn't that Harlem's middle name, Rose?" Manny asked.

"Yes, Harlem's father must have thought a lot of his mother to give Harlem her name," Sister Delores said.

"Apparently, Belinda felt that David's body should be with his family. She gave her permission for David to be sent back to Kolter with strict confidentiality that his parents were not to be told of his marriage. She told the authorities that in due time she would let them know about the marriage when she thought they would be ready to accept her and her child," Manny said.

"Manny, for almost nine years they had a grandchild and didn't know about her. Maybe Harlem's life would have been different. I guess you can't look back at what could have been. Hopefully, she can start a new chapter in her life with her grandfather. All we can do is hope that he is capable of taking care of her and capable of loving her and being a big part of the family she deserves."

"I was told Harlem will be going by bus. I'll know some time today when they call me back the exact day and time she will be leaving for Kolter," Manny said.

"She will be all by herself on the bus Manny. That is a long trip. I am worried about that."

"I'll take care of making sure she is taken care of Sister Delores. Don't worry about that. Maybe you better break the news to her. I hope she takes it well."

"I'll tell her after supper tonight," Sister Delores replied.

"I'll let you know if I hear anymore. Sister Delores, don't look so sad. She deserves a family of her own. She has the chance to know and have a family that neither one of us had," Manny said.

"I know, I know. You go now. I don't want you to miss that phone call," Sister Delores said.

That night after supper, Harlem helped Sister Rachael carry the dishes into the kitchen to be washed. Her duty usually was to dry the dishes and Sister Jean would put them away. Sister Delores didn't get to eat very much. She had to run over to the church vestibule because she had an important call from Officer Lopez that she had been apprehensively waiting for.

This night was different. After Sister Delores came back into the convent, she asked Harlem to come into the sitting room to have a talk with her. Harlem thought, "oh boy, I got out of drying all those dishes and pots and pans tonight."

"Harlem, the phone call I just got was from Officer Lopez. I'm going to try to explain this to you the best way I can. You know how all these months special people have been trying to find a family member of yours?" Sister Delores said.

With somewhat of a puzzled look Harlem said, "yes ma'am. Did they find somebody?"

"Yes Harlem, and the person they found is a very special relative. Your grandfather was found. What do you think of that?"

"I don't understand. Why didn't he come to see me all these years? Do I have a grandmother?" Harlem asked.

"From what I understand, your grandfather didn't know about you. Your mother didn't tell him. And as far as your grandmother, sadly, she passed away right after your father died. Maybe one day when you get older, everything will make sense to you and you will understand why things happened the way they did," Sister Delores replied.

"Why wouldn't my mother let my grandfather and grandmother know about me? Was she ashamed of something I did?" Harlem asked.

"No, no, no! Nothing was your fault. Maybe she was afraid after your father died that they would take you away from her. Her life and her job were here. Harlem, forget about the past. You have a chance that a lot of children never have. Some children never get to have a real family. I told you before; don't dwell on the past and what should have been. Think about the future and what goodness you can contribute to this world," Sister Delores said.

"So where in New York does my grandfather live, and is he coming here to visit with me?"

"Your grandfather lives many hours away from here in a small mountain town in West Virginia called Kolter. Harlem, Father Dominic was told by the archdiocese that you can't stay here any longer. We all are very sad over this, but there is nothing we can do. I tried everything I could to keep you here. We love you Harlem. There was no way I was going to let Father Dominic put you in a foster home. So we tried very hard and were very lucky to find your grandfather," Sister Delores replied.

"So I have to leave. I don't want to. Please Sister Delores, please let me stay!" Harlem started crying.

"Harlem the only thing I can do is pack a bag and you and I can run away tonight. I don't know where we would go. If that would make you happy, I am willing to leave this school and convent and go tonight," Sister Delores said trying to comfort Harlem.

"You would do that for me?" Harlem asked.

"Yes, I would. You just let me know when you want to leave and we will leave," Sister Delores replied.

"What about all the kids? Who's going to teach the third grade? What about the sisters? They're going to be sad and miss you and won't know what to do," Harlem said.

Sister Delores replied, "they will get along fine without me."

"No, they won't. They need you. You can't go. I'll go, but if I don't like it there, I'm running away."

"You will not run away Harlem Rose." Sister Delores said sternly. "You will stay and do your best to try to adjust to your new surroundings just like you did here at the convent. If you are mistreated by your grandfather, that is different. In that case, you call Officer Lopez or me and one of us will be there to bring you back here. We'll try extra hard to find you a nice family to live with. Now promise me you won't run away and you will call one of us!"

Harlem hangs her head down. "Yes ma'am, I will. When do I have to leave?"

"You have to leave the day after tomorrow. There was nothing I could do about that either Harlem. Officer Lopez and I will take you to the bus terminal to see you off."

"I'm really going to miss you, the other sisters and my friends here at school, especially Arlene."

"I know, I know. Just make sure you have all the addresses and phone numbers written down and put them where you can find them. And the convent phone will be fixed tomorrow, I made sure of that. You know that number by heart. You just call me any time for anything. I will always be there for you Harlem."

"I know you will Sister Delores." Harlem looks up at Sister Delores. "I wish you could be my new mother."

Tears filled Sister Delores' eyes. She didn't want Harlem to see that. She looked away while hugging Harlem and said, "so do I, so do I."

chapter 12

THE DREADED DAY had finally arrived. Officer Lopez picked Sister Delores and Harlem up at the convent and drove the short distance to the bus terminal. It was a cloudy, bitterly cold February day, accompanied by bouts of cold rain. There was an atmosphere of sadness in the squad car.

The nasty weather didn't halt the number of people traveling that morning. Harlem's bus wasn't that crowded. Not those many people were traveling to West Virginia. There were a lot of Florida bound passengers on the other buses. The three of them walked over to Harlem's bus.

"Harlem, remember what I said. If things don't work out you have the phone numbers and addresses of people to contact. Sister Rachael packed you at least three sandwiches, cookies and milk. Now you write me as soon as you can."

"I will Sister Delores. Maybe you and the sisters can come and see me."

"That's a good idea. We haven't had a vacation from the convent in years. We will mail the rest of your belongings, so be looking for them Harlem. Harlem, don't forget to find that special place for your mother's ashes."

"I will. Good-bye Sister Delores."

"Good-bye Harlem. I love you."

Officer Lopez proceeded to put Harlem and her suitcase on the bus.

"Sit up here by the bus driver Harlem. He can keep an eye on you. Don't be so sad, I have an excuse now to visit West Virginia," Officer Lopez said.

Officer Lopez stepped off the bus and the bus driver was getting on the bus.

Officer Lopez heard the words "get in the back little girl". The voice sounded like the bus drivers voice.

Officer Lopez, hurriedly, jumped back on the bus and saw Harlem moving to the last seat on the bus.

"Harlem, get back up front. Why are you going all the way to the back of the bus?" Officer Lopez asked.

"The bus driver told me to," Harlem replied.

Officer Lopez turned to the bus driver and said, "can you leave the bus for a minute so we can a few words?"

"One minute officer that's all I can give you. I'm on a schedule," the bus driver said.

"Why did you tell her to go to the back of the bus? She's just a little girl," Officer Lopez asked.

"She's also colored. I'm picking up passengers along the way that are going further south. You know what I mean?" the bus driver said.

Officer Lopez grabbed the bus driver by the front of his jacket and pushed him against the bus and said, "no, you listen to me. That little girl is going to ride up front with you. You are going to keep an eye on her the whole trip. If you stop at a rest stop, you will make sure she goes to the restroom and gets safely back on the bus again. You're responsible for her from here to Kolter, West Virginia until her grandfather can pick her up at the bus terminal. If I find out you didn't look after her, you better take this bus and drive it to Mars. You got that!!"

"Yeah, yeah, I got it," replied the bus driver.

The bus driver got back on the bus and told Harlem to sit in the front seat.

"Well, Officer Lopez, I mean Manny, I don't think I have to worry about Harlem's bus trip," Sister Delores said with a big smile on her face.

The bus finally pulled out. Harlem was waving to Officer Lopez and Sister Delores as they waved back to her.

Harlem's new chapter in her life was about to commence.

chapter 13

THE MORNING BOONE Jackson left for his old friend Brady O'Brannan's house on top of old Kolter Mountain, he stopped at the local country store, Tyler's Grocery Market. Mr. Ron Tyler, the owner and post master of the small post office in the back of the store, handed him two very important telegrams. One telegram was from the Department of Missing Persons in Washington D.C. and the other telegram was from Child Welfare Services in New York City.

"Boone, these two sealed telegrams have been lyin' around here for a few days. They're marked URGENT. They were delivered special delivery from the main post office in Morgantown. They are for Brady and he very seldom ever comes to town much less stops by here and picks up his mail. Can you be my special delivery man this mornin' and take them up the mountain to him? I'll give you five cents off on any brand of chewin' tobacco you want."

"Sure will Ron. I'm headin' that way anyway. Brady's got a lumber shipment to get out and needs my help. I'll take them, and I want some of that chewin' tobacco you just got in. Think I'll try that new brand, and I'll take you at your word about that five cents off," Boone said.

"Now if I'd known you were goin' that way, I wouldn't have made that good offer. Seein' how I am a man of my word, you're goin' to get that five cents off," Ron Tyler replied.

"Thank you Ron. You're a good man no matter what the folks say about you around these parts."

Ron jokingly said, "you better get goin' Boone before I change my mind and charge you an extra five cents."

Boone was somewhat of a spectacle in the small town of Kolter. He was who he was and didn't care what the people in town thought of him. He wore a coonskin hat, buckskin jacket and buckskin boots. He shot the coon and the buck himself and made his own hat, jacket and boots. He did cut his gray hair himself but kept it shoulder length and it was as unkempt as his beard. He took a bath once a week whether he needed it or not and he had one best friend, Brady O'Brannan.

Boone couldn't climb old Kolter Mountain fast enough in that old rickety Ford farm truck he was driving. The deep snow and ice grabbed his tires and almost made him slide off of the side of the mountain on every curve he took. The road was only big enough for one vehicle. If someone was coming from the other direction, one of the drivers would have to back all the way down the mountain or hang off the edge and hope for the best. Boone knew for sure no one would be coming because the only person who lived on the very top of the mountain was Brady O'Brannan, and he never got any visitors except Boone.

Every time one of Boone's tires would slip going around a sharp tight curve, he would curse Brady. "Damn you Brady O'Brannan". He would then roll his window down and spit his chewing tobacco out. The only problem was the cold northern winds blowing through the pines would blow part of that disgusting tobacco back into his already unkempt, scraggly gray beard.

As Boone took the last sharp curve up that treacherous mountain road to Brady's house he said to himself, "urgent! Who in the world is sendin' Brady somethin' urgent from Washington D.C. and New York too?"

When Boone pulled up to Brady's home, he noticed Brady's truck was there. He wasn't in the barn or the work shed sawing any new timber. He knocked once and went inside the house, but Brady wasn't anywhere to be found. The only one present was Gladys, his pet hen who just laid an egg on the kitchen floor. "Get, get outside Gladys, get. I don't know why we ain't had you for dinner yet. Brady must be gettin' soft in his old age."

Boone hollered for Blue Boy, Brady's pride and joy – his dog, a Border Collie, and smart as a whip. He could hear the barking in the distant woods and worried for a minute that Brady may be hurt. Boone followed the footprints in the snow to the very top of Kolter Mountain.

This was Brady's favorite spot. The very top of the mountain over-looked the beautiful hills and valleys below with the old cabins in the hollers and open fields and farms with cows and horses. Even though it was freezing and sleeting on and off, Brady would just stare off into that wilderness surrounded by tall oaks, hickories, balsam fir, hemlock and Christmas fern. How beautiful the woods looked when the snow glistened on the leaves of the trees.

The O'Brannan family cemetery was also on top of that mountain. There were several members of the O'Brannan family buried there. Kathleen, Brady's wife and his son David were the last two to be buried in the cemetery. Brady was sitting on a bench he built that sat in front of his wife's grave. There was a wreath Brady had made out of pine tips that he had placed on Kathleen's grave. Blue Boy was lying at his feet but got up right away to welcome Boone.

"Been a long time Brady. Kathleen Rose and David have been gone a long time," Boone said.

"Don't tell me nothin' I don't already know Boone. Just tell me how I'am supposed to get up every day knowin' she's not goin' to be there. She never should have died Boone. We had so much more we planned to do together."

"You know she was real sick Brady."

"No, she got sick when she found out David went into the service. He never came home again. When he did come home, he was in a box and we had to bury him. Boone, she died of a broken heart. I never could forgive him. Ain't right what he did to his mama. No word from him, nothin'," Brady said.

"You got to get over that Brady, he was your boy. He was a good boy too. You and him just butted heads. You got to forgive him Brady," Boone said.

"Don't you think I knew we didn't see eye to eye Boone? I just can't forgive him right now. I just can't. I don't want to talk about it no more," Brady said.

"Ok we won't talk about it no more. But there's somethin' you got to read Brady. Got it here in my pocket. When I stopped by the store this mornin', Ron gave me these here telegrams for you to read. They're marked urgent. One is from Washington D.C. and the other from New York City."

"You can tear them up. I don't know anybody from Washington or New York," Brady said.

"Well, since I'm goin' to tear them up, do you mind if I read them? Could be Brady, you're our new President. Wouldn't you like to know if you are?" Boone said laughing.

"Sure, you can read them out loud. We can both get a few laughs," Brady said.

Boone knew that Brady couldn't read very well. He respected Brady too much to say anything to hurt him. They played this little game with the mail quite often. But down deep inside Brady felt that Boone knew his little secret. Nobody in town ever found out Brady couldn't read, because his good friend Boone did most of the paper-work for his lumber business.

"Here goes." Boone opens the first telegram from Washington D.C.

Mr. Brady O'Brannan We are informing you that you have an 8 year old Granddaughter, Harlem Rose O'Brannan. Stop...Her mother has died and you are her only next-of-kin. Stop...She has been staying at St. Anthony's in a convent- for several months in Bronx NY. Stop. She will be traveling by bus to Kolter, West Virginia within a few days to live with you...stop You will be notified when she will be leaving NY and when she will arrive in Kolter, West Virginia by the Child Welfare Services Dept.

Bureau of Missing Persons, Washington D.C.

Boone's eyes got big, but Brady's even got bigger.

"What am I supposed to do with a granddaughter? How do I know she belongs to David? Boone you've got to go into town with me. I got to send a telegram back and tell them I don't want her here. I can't raise a little girl. I don't want to raise anybody. Come on, let's go!"

"Wait a minute. I better read this other telegram before we do anything," Boone said.

Boone starts reading the telegram from Child Welfare Services.

Mr. Brady O'Brannan:

Harlem Rose O'Brannan will be arriving February 5th at approximately 5 o'clock in the afternoon from Bronx, New York at the Kolter, West Virginia bus terminal. Stop

Please be there to pick up your granddaughter.

NY Child Welfare Services Dept.

"Come on Boone, let's go. I got to stop this."

"Brady, do you know what today is? It's the fourth of February. It's too late. She is probably on the bus already. You're going to have to pick her up tomorrow. You ain't got no choice son," Boone said.

"You're wrong, I got a choice. I don't want her here. What can't you understand? I'm goin' down the mountain now and tell the manager at the bus terminal to leave her on that bus, turn it around and send it back to New York. Ain't nobody goin' to tell Brady O'Brannan what he can and can't do."

"Don't you even want to meet your granddaughter Brady? She's part of David. That makes her part of you and Kathleen. She has Kathleen's middle name Rose. David thought so much of his mama that he gave his daughter her name. Doesn't that count for somethin'? She might even remind you of your Kathleen."

"No, leave it go Boone. David didn't think enough of us to let us know he was married. Then he has this baby and didn't tell us. It's almost been nine years Boone. Why didn't his wife try to contact us after he died? What kind of woman was she?"

"You really don't know the "whys" right now Brady. This lady had her reasons why she didn't contact you. Maybe she thought David didn't have any parents. Did you ever think of that?"

"If that is what happened, then it is David's fault Kathleen died way too early. Kathleen always wanted more children. She would have loved that baby too death. You know how tender-hearted she was. If she would have known at the time he had a baby, things might have been different. She would have had a reason to go on," Brady said.

"Brady, you don't know that. She was a very sick woman. Knowin' about this little girl might have made her a little happier, but I don't think it would have helped her stay in this world any longer."

"That's your opinion, Boone, and you can keep it to yourself. I'm not going tomorrow and that's all there is to it."

"You're bull-headed. Now I know why David and you butted heads. I know the real Brady and he would never hurt any creature that roamed this mountain. So how can you turn your back on your flesh and blood?"

Brady replied, "she needs a grandma not a grandpa. She's used to city life. What am I going to do with her here in these rugged mountains full of bear, bobcats, timber wolves and you know all the rest?"

"I think you're scared. Yep. A big, strong mountain man scared of a little bitty girl," Boone said.

"If you weren't my best friend, I'd lay you out cold right here and let the wolves carry your hide away," Brady said.

Boone said, "well I sure am glad I'm your best friend. Hate to see what you would do to me if you didn't like me. Now let's think this through. Why can't you just meet her? If you don't like her, put her back on the bus, get in your truck and skedaddle out of town and back up here. You know nobody ever comes up here 'cept me. People just ain't afraid of the mountain, they're afraid of you."

"You callin' me a coward Boone Jackson?"

Boone backs away. "No, no, I'm just offerin' my advice on how you can handle the situation."

"I'm no coward. I don't run from any situation much less a little girl. We're goin' tomorrow to pick her up. Now let's get this lumber delivered," Brady said.

Snickering a little, Boone looked at Brady and said, "you're right Brady. You're doin' the right thing, but don't you think we better clean the house a little and fix David's room for the little girl before tomorrow. You want to make a good impression now, don't you?"

"Ok, but you're goin' to help me seein' how you're makin' me feel like a big ole' daddy bear that just ate its cub," Brady said.

"Come on daddy bear, we got a lot to do before that bus pulls in at 5 o'clock."

chapter 14

BRADY, BOONE AND Blue Boy arrived about an hour early at the bus station in Kolter the next day to meet Harlem when the bus arrived.

Brady looked handsome in his black leather cowboy hat, black buckskin jacket with fringes on the sleeves, denim overalls and light blue dress shirt with a bola tie made from turquoise and silver. The bola tie was a gift handed down from the Cherokee Chief to his great-great grandfather when his family came to America from Ireland to settle in the mountains of Kolter years ago.

"You're really lookin' like a 'city slicker' today Brady, but when you goin' to cut that pigtail or whatever you call that hair hangin' down your back?"

"I ain't cutin' nothin'. If you got a problem with the way I look, get out of the truck now and sit on the pile of snow across the road and freeze your 'hind-end' off."

"Come on Brady. I'm just lookin' out for you. I thought maybe the women folk might look at you a little bit more if you cut off that old pigtail. A big strapin' guy like you should have more of a haircut like . . . like me. The ladies seem to like it."

"Bein' interested in a woman is the last thing on my mind. I had the best, and have you really looked in the mirror lately Boone? On second thought maybe you better not, you might scare yourself."

"Now that's not a nice thing to tell your best friend Brady. I get a lot of winks from the ladies, especially when I go in Ron's grocery store. Anyway I know a little gal that asks me about you all the time."

"Ok, who is it? You're not goin' to quit until I ask."

"Remember Jesse Mason? We cut and delivered all the lumber for his barn last summer," Boone said.

"Yeah, why?" Brady asked.

"Well I ran into his daughter Sara a few times in town and she always asks about you. She is a teacher at Kolter Elementary, and she's sure a pretty little thing."

"What is she fifteen, Boone?"

"No she ain't no fifteen. She's near close to forty and prettier than any woman that lives in these parts. She's a little bit of a lady with long blonde hair and her skin looks as fresh and pretty as a peach just picked off a tree. Her daddy told me she was married once to a vacuum cleaner salesman. He ran off with some gal in Harper's Ferry and never came back. She went and got a divorce and moved back in with her daddy and mama. It broke her heart. That's what Jesse told me."

"It's a sad story Boone, but I'm not interested. You know you're nosier than those ladies at the Friday night cattle auctions across from Hickory Creek. They sit at a table in the corner and talk about everybody that walks through the door while they're sippin' a little moonshine out of a coke bottle. You should sit with them instead of me the next time we go," Brady said.

"Brady, I'm just lookin' out for you, especially since your gettin' a new family member. A woman's touch is always appreciated and you ain't gettin' any younger. You're gone to be fifty pretty soon, or did you forget?"

"No I ain't forgot, and I ain't ready for the boneyard either. So just get all that out of your head. Boone … here comes the bus. I'm kinda' gettin' a little nervous now. I feel like I want to turn around, and take off."

"Brady, you better not. Now come on boy, it's goin' to be ok. Just be the Brady you've always been. Come on. Let's get out of the truck and wait for her to get off the bus."

"We don't even know what she looks like Boone. I don't want to grab some little girl and she starts screamin'."

"You don't grab nobody Brady. You walk up and introduce yourself as Brady O'Brannan. That's all there is to it. Come on, let's go."

There weren't many people standing around waiting for the bus to discharge passengers. Brady and Boone watched every person who got off the bus, but there were no little girls leaving the bus. It looked as if the last passenger just exited the bus. The bus driver had not stepped off the bus yet.

"Boone, you think those child welfare people got the time or bus terminal mixed up? What do we do now?"

"Don't jump to no conclusions now Brady. Let's go over and talk to the bus driver. He's gettin' off the bus now."

As Boone and Brady walked toward the bus driver, he walked toward them.

Brady confronted the bus driver and said, "sir, is there a little girl on the bus or was a little girl on the bus and she got off at another stop?"

The bus driver stepped aside and said, "you mean this little girl. I was given strict orders in New York not to let her out of my sight until she was handed over to a Mr. Brady O'Brannan. Is that you?"

Boone and Brady didn't know what to say. They imagined David's child would be a little blonde-haired, fair-skinned child. Instead a little light brown girl with light brown hair was standing in front of them. They both knew that this little girl is colored, she couldn't belong to David.

Brady in a puzzling voice asked the bus driver. "Are you sure there wasn't another little girl on the bus and she got off at the wrong stop?"

The bus driver in a tired but adamant voice told Brady, "Mr., I have been on the road since yesterday afternoon. I got threatened by a police officer before I even left New York and I am tired, dead tired. Little girl tell this nice man who you are."

Harlem peeked around the bus driver and looked up at this huge man dressed like the cowboys she read about in her history books. She was quite intimidated and scared at the same time. She thought Sister Delores was scary until she really got to know her. She looked straight up at Brady and said, "my name is Harlem ... Harlem Rose O'Brannan. Are you my grandfather?"

Boone nudged Brady because he just stood there staring at Harlem and didn't say anything. "Brady, the little girl is askin' you a question. Aren't you goin' to answer her and introduce me?"

Brady looked down at Harlem and said, "I guess I am your grandfather if your name is Harlem Rose O'Brannan."

Not knowing what to do, and not being a man to show his feelings, Brady held his hand out and shook hands with Harlem. "Nice to meet you Harlem Rose O'Brannan."

The bus driver looked up at Brady and said, "I'm not here for the family reunion. I'm out of here. Good luck Mr."

Brady introduced Boone to Harlem. "Harlem, this here is my friend Boone Jackson."

Harlem looked up at Boone with a smile and said, "glad to meet you Mr. Jackson."

"Did you hear that Brady, she called me Mr. Jackson? She knows a gentleman when she meets one. You don't have to call me Mr. Jackson. You call me Boone like everybody else, ok? And I'm his best friend, not just his friend."

"Ok Mr. Boone, I'll still call you Mr. Boone. Are you related to Daniel Boone?"

"Well as a matter of fact, I was told I was named Boone after Daniel Boone on my mother's side. My mother married a Jackson."

"Boone, stop pullin' her leg. You know that ain't a true fact."

Harlem picks her leg up. "He's not pulling my leg, see."

Brady looked down at her and said, "I don't mean he is really pullin' your leg, I mean he might be tellin' a little white lie."

Harlem looked at Boone and said, "Mr. Boone, if you really don't know what the truth is, you shouldn't lie. If Sister Delores were here, she would make you go to confession."

"What's she talkin' about Brady, confession? And I ain't tellin' no white lie. They were true facts passed down from the Jackson family."

Brady just shakes his head at Boone and asks Harlem. "Are you hungry Harlem? It's supper time. I know I am and I'm sure Boone is."

"Yeah, I sure am hungry grand . . . What should I call you?"

"You can call me Brady like everybody else if you want to."

"But you're my grandfather, and that's not respectful," Harlem said.

"Did you hear that Brady, she's not only pretty and bright but real respectful too," Boone said.

"Ok, how about grandpa. That's what I called my grandfather," Brady replied.

"Then let's eat Grandpa, I'm starving."

"Ok, we'll go right down the road to Dave & Mary's restaurant. They serve some good down home cookin' there. Most folk around here eat there," Brady said.

When Brady opened the truck door, Blue Boy jumped out and jumped all over Harlem. It was love at first sight between both of them. Harlem was so excited to be able to pet this dog. She couldn't have a dog in her apartment in the projects and would never be allowed to have one in the convent.

Boone looked at Brady and said, "Blue Boy don't take to everybody like that Brady. That's unusual. Animals got that special instinct to know and trust good folk."

"I know all about animals and their instincts Boone. Now let's get gone. I can eat a whole cow now. Sorry Blue Boy, you have to get in the back until we get to the restaurant, then you can get back up front."

Harlem spoke up and said, "oh no, it's too cold for him in the back of the truck. He can sit on my lap."

Boone said, "you sure Harlem, he is kind of big?"

"That's ok, I want to hold him. I can't wait to write to my friend Arlene and tell her about my new dog. Is that ok with you Grandpa, that I tell her I have a dog?"

"Sure is ok. The way he took to you."

Brady and Boone just looked at each other and a little smile appeared on Brady's face. A little smile that Boone had not seen on his face for years.

chapter 15

IT WAS A little after six o'clock when Brady, Boone and Harlem arrived at Dave & Mary's restaurant, and there were quite a few cars in the parking lot. It was supper time and crowded. The crowd consisted of several of the town's people in Kolter. Everybody knew each other and this was the gathering place, especially on Friday night after work.

When Brady, Boone and Harlem walked through the door to the restaurant, the loud talking and laughing from the patrons eating super came almost to a hush. The loudest sounds were from the juke box with Jim Reeves singing "Four Walls". The three of them sat down in a booth and waited for their menus so they could order their meal. Brady and Boone had frequented the restaurant several times and knew the owners quite well. The restaurant was built with timber that Brady cut from his property on top of Kolter Mountain. He even allowed Dave and Mary to pay him at a reduced rate whatever they could. As a matter of fact they still owed Brady money after all these years and he told them to forget it. Brady also donated all the timber for the First Christian Church of Kolter, which is the church where most of the people in the restaurant attended on Sundays.

Harlem leaned over to Brady and whispered in an excited voice, "Grandpa, I've never been in a restaurant before."

Brady said, "you're in one now little girl."

Both Brady and Boone sensed something was wrong when the talking in the restaurant subsided.

Mary walked over, but without any menus. "Brady, Dave wants to talk to you if you have a second."

"Sure, tell him I'll be right there. Keep an eye on Harlem, Boone."

"Won't take my eyes off of her Brady."

Brady walked down towards the kitchen door where Dave was standing.

"What's the problem Dave?" Brady asked.

"Brady, I know you been a good friend and helped me with this restaurant and everything, but I have to look out for my business. I can't afford to lose customers."

"So what are you tryin' to tell me Dave?"

"Just look at that sign on the wall Brady – over there. It says NO COLORED ALLOWED. That little girl you brought in here, she's colored. You and Boone can stay and get waited on but she has to go."

Brady's face got red. He clenched his fists. Boone could see something was wrong. Boone got up and came over and stood beside Brady.

"Brady what's wrong?" Boone asked.

"Boone did you ever notice that sign on the wall over there?"

"What sign?" Then Boone looks up and sees the NO COLORED ALLOWED sign.

"Never did notice it before Brady. What are we going to do about it?" Boone asked.

Brady backs Dave up against the wall so the people in the restaurant can't hear him and said, "what am I goin' to do Boone. I'm goin' to tear the sign down along with every piece of timber in this place that that I cut from my property up on Kolter Mountain."

Dave backed up against the wall and said, "you can't do that, I paid you for some of this timber."

"Oh, I know you did Dave. I'm not takin' down the pieces you paid for, just the ones you didn't pay for."

Dave said, "I'll just call the sheriff."

"You go right ahead Dave and call the sheriff. I still have that note that states you owe me money. I'll own this restaurant tonight."

"Ok, ok, Mary give them a menu!"

Brady looked at Dave and said, "I wouldn't eat here if you paid me. Come on Boone. I found out what slimy back-stabbin' people run this place. And by the way Dave, that little colored girl is my granddaughter."

"Brady, I'm sorry. I'm sor . . ."

"Too late Dave. All the sorry's in the world aren't going to change this day. Now I know what kind of person and coward you are to turn a little kid away that's hungry and supposedly two good friends. That's all I needed to know about you."

After Brady and Boone turn their backs and started to walk away, Dave said, "I didn't turn my back on you and Boone. I just said the little girl couldn't eat here."

Dave should have kept his mouth shut, because he made things worse by saying that.

Brady turned around and started back while Dave ran into the kitchen. Boone had to hold Brady back and that wasn't easy.

Boone said, "Brady, Brady, don't do somethin' you're goin' to be sorry for later. You got a little granddaughter sittin' in that booth wonderin' what's goin' on. You don't want her to know do you?"

After Boone calmed Brady down, the three of them walked out of the restaurant. Boone turned around and walked back in. He went over to the sign and tore it down, threw it down on the floor, did a little dance on it and walked out and slammed the door.

There was silence as the three of them and Blue Boy sat in the truck. Brady was so furious he sat at the steering wheel with his fists still clenched. Boone knew better than to say a word when Brady was in that state of mind.

"Boone, you wait here with Harlem. I'm goin' to go in and have another talk with Dave."

"Now Brady, just sit here for a few minutes and calm yourself down. You've got somebody else besides yourself to think about now. You don't want to wind up you know where tonight, do you?"

"Maybe you're right. But I ain't forgettin' tonight."

"We both know you ain't a man that forgets. Remember yesterday when we had our talk about the "whys"? Now you know why things happened the way they did a long time ago," Boone said.

Brady replied, "let's just drop this Boone. Somebody, and we both know who I'm talkin' about should have had a lot more trust in me."

"Grandpa, you know I'm really not that hungry. Do you have some milk or a can of tomato soup at your house? That will fill me up tonight. I don't want you to wind up "you know where tonight" either."

"Dag nab it, she sure is a smart little thing, ain't she Brady?"

"That's because she's my granddaughter and an O'Brannan, Boone."

While all three were laughing at what Harlem said, there was a knock on Boone's window.

Boone rolls his window down. "Sara, Sara Mason. Brady this is the little lady I was tellin' you about earlier. Girl, it's too cold out there for you to stand. Let's switch places."

"I'm only going to be a minute Boone. I couldn't help overhearing what happened in the restaurant. I just wanted to let you know that I'm sorry. But there is another restaurant at the end of town. It's called "Mama Lucille's Place". They've got the best fried chicken and dumplings in town, better than Dave's. Just make sure you tell her Sara sent you and you all are friends of mine."

Forgetting that Harlem is in the truck, Boone asks Sara. "You sure Sara. I thought that place just served col . . . folk."

Brady hits Boone in the shoulder. "Boone, watch what you're sayin'. We appreciate it Miss Sara because we sure are hungry."

"Brady, please don't call me Miss Sara, just Sara. And Boone there aren't any restrictions in Mama Lucille's restaurant. And who is this pretty little girl?"

"I'm Brady O'Brannan's granddaughter. My name is Harlem. Brady is my grandpa."

"Nice to meet you Harlem," Sara said.

"Nice to meet you too, Miss Sara," Harlem said.

"Oh my, the snow is starting to come down again and I better get going home or my parents will be worried about me. And Brady, I don't know if you thought anything about it yet and I know it is none of my business, but maybe you should think about enrolling Harlem in school. Well, I have to go. Bye everybody," Sara said.

Brady, Boone and Harlem all say good-bye to Sara.

"Didn't I tell you Brady how pretty she was?" Boone said.

"Yes, you did Boone. She sure is pretty and nice too," Brady replied.

"I like her Grandpa. I hope I get to see her again."

Brady just smiled and said, "Harlem, I'm pretty sure we'll be seein' her again."

Mama Lucille's restaurant was at the very end of town in the colored section. The three of them were welcomed into her restaurant, and ate the best fried chicken and dumplings they ever tasted. All they had to do was tell Miss Lucille that they were friends of Sara's and they were treated very well.

Brady noticed the run down condition of the restaurant, but most of the colored folks didn't get paid the same or get the good jobs like the white folks in Kolter. The restaurant was clean and the food was a lot better than the food at Dave and Mary's restaurant. This is the place that he, Boone and Harlem would be coming from now on. That was a sure thing.

Brady was curious as to how Sara knew Miss Lucille and why she even visited that part of town. He found out from Miss Lucille that two nights a week Sara teaches reading to a lot of the colored folks in the back of the restaurant for free. Miss Lucille also insisted Brady not mentioned this to anyone because the town's people might not accept what Sara is doing and put a stop to it or give her a hard time.

Brady thought to himself, "this little lady, Sara, has a big, ole' warm heart. She reminds me a lot of Kathleen."

chapter 16

IT WAS PRETTY late and very dark when Brady drove back home. Harlem couldn't get over the long winding trip around the mountains to get to Brady's house. Harlem fell asleep with her head resting on Blue Boy and Blue Boy was partially lying on Boone. The snow was starting to fall again and it was getting very cold. The north wind howled through the mountains. It sounded like a train was following the truck. Brady finally pulled up in front of his house.

"Here we are. Finally home. You got to wake up, Harlem. Boone, you take Harlem inside while I get her suitcase and bring some wood in for a fire," Brady said.

When Boone opened the door, Gladys ran out and startled Harlem.

"Mr. Boone, what was that?"

"Harlem, ain't you ever seen a hen before?"

"No sir, just in books that I have read."

"Well, this one don't belong in here, but Brady spoiled her. Your grandpa calls her Gladys. So you keep her outside in her own little house. She needs to know she is just a chicken not a person."

"But she is so cute Mr. Boone. Look!! There is a big brown egg on the floor over there."

Harlem picks the egg up and holds it like she has never seen an egg before.

"Girl, ain't you ever seen an egg before?" Boone laughed.

"Yes sir. But not one that a hen just layed."

"Harlem, you got a lot of surprises in store for you here in these ole' mountains if that there egg shocks you that much. It's a whole new world up here in these mountains. Yes sir, it sure is. I forgot you were a city girl. What it was like livin' in a big city like New York?"

Just then Brady comes in with the wood and starts the fire and listens as Harlem proceeds to describe to Boone what her city life was like.

"My mama and I lived in an apartment building in the projects in Bronx, New York."

Boone asks, "what's the projects?"

"It's a whole bunch of apartments on top of each other. There is this real high fence around all of them," Harlem replies.

Boone said, "that sounds like prison to me. Where in the world did you play?"

"Mama wouldn't let me play outside because there were bad people with guns shooting all the time."

Brady just stood back where Harlem couldn't see him and listened as he fired up the logs.

Boone looked at Harlem and said, "sounds like your mama was a pretty smart lady to me."

"My mama was real smart. She was a LPN; that means licensed practical nurse. She was going to school at night to be a registered nurse. Walking home from school one night somebody from a gang shot at somebody else and it missed them and hit my mama."

Harlem stopped talking and looked down at the floor then turned around to Brady and said, "can I go to bed now Grandpa, I'm really tired?"

"Sure you can Harlem. Let me show you where you will be sleepin' and where you can put your things."

Brady took Harlem into David's old bedroom.

"Harlem, this is where your Daddy used to sleep when he was a little boy."

Harlem started crying and took the only picture she had of her parents and her as an infant out of her suitcase and set it on the dresser.

Brady was shocked. This was a picture of his son, David, two months before he died and he was holding Harlem.

"Your mama was a pretty lady Harlem. Sounds to me like you were everything in the world to her," Brady said.

Harlem still crying, "she wanted to be a registered nurse so we could move out of the projects and buy a nice house out of the city. She was scared for me and wanted me out of there. I was going to be a doctor one day and give her everything that she could never have, but things didn't turn out that way."

With no one looking, Brady grabbed Harlem and hugged her. "She was a good lady Harlem, and you can still be that doctor you want to be. We sure could use a good one here in Kolter. Come on, get in bed. I've got a lot to show you tomorrow. Night Harlem."

"Goodnight Grandpa. I love you."

Brady just couldn't get those words 'I love you too' out of his mouth. That just wasn't him. The people that he had loved were taken away from him. He was known around town as a strong mountain man with this tough exterior, who had very little to say. He kept the compassionate side of his personality from others, except of course from his best friend Boone who knew Brady as well as his long-deceased mother did. Brady was afraid to let his guard down even though no one was looking. He could see, with this little girl, that he wasn't going to be able to portray that overly tough guy image for too much longer.

When he came out of her bedroom, Brady noticed that Boone was wiping a tear from his eye. "Boone Jackson, is that a tear I see runnin' down that ugly face of yours?"

"No, it ain't. I got a cold in my right eye and I ain't got a ugly face."

"Why don't you stay here tonight or for a couple of days? The weather is bad Boone. You know where the cot is in the attic."

"Thanks Brady. That little girl has lost everybody in her family. All she's got now is you. At least in these here mountains she can run and play and do what she wants without worryin' 'bout gettin' shot. You're doin' a good thing Brady."

"All go on and go to bed Boone before I toss you out the door and you'll have to sleep in the snow," Brady said.

"Oh, before I go up to the attic I want to ask you an important question. Do you think you better take Harlem to school and enroll her? She's a smart little girl. It would be a shame not to let her go," Boone said.

"I thought about it Boone. She said she wants to be a doctor one day. Doctor school costs a lot of money. I'm gone to have to cut a lot of wood and sell a lot more of it to save for her to go to college."

"Brady, you can count on me to help you. See you in the mornin'."

The next morning Harlem was excited to start the new day with her grandpa. What really woke her up was the smell of bacon cooking. The aroma magically filled the house and called her name. She hurriedly got dressed and ran down the steep steps to the small kitchen to see Boone, with an apron on, cooking breakfast.

"Mr. Boone that sure smells good," Harlem said.

"Well little lady guess who I'm cookin' this for?" Boone asked.

"For me."

"Darn tootin' it's for you. Remember that egg Gladys laid on the floor last night?" Boone asked.

"Yes sir, I do," Harlem replied.

"Here it is. Special delivery with three slices of the best bacon this side of West Virginia you're ever goin' to taste," Boone said.

"Thank you, Mr. Boone!"

While Harlem was eating, she asked Boone. "Where is Grandpa?"

"He's further on up the mountain cuttin' some timber for a cabin bein' built by some rich tourist down in the valley close to McSchowell County."

Boone sat down to eat with Harlem.

"After we eat breakfast, Mr. Boone, can you take me where Grandpa is so I can watch him cut timber?"

"I guess it will be ok with your Grandpa, but you better dress real warm because it is really cold outside."

"Oh, I got new boots, gloves, leggings and a nice coat for Christmas. I won't be cold."

"Ok as soon as you chow that breakfast down, we'll go."

Harlem takes the last big bite. "Done. Let's go!!"

Harlem didn't get to see much of the mountain in the dark. This was a chance for her to really get a good look at everything during the day especially since they were taking their time walking up the mountain.

"Mr. Boone, it's so beautiful. Does Grandpa own all this land?"

"Yes, ma'am, he sure does."

"I wish my friend Arlene could see this. I have all this (she spins around) land to play in and I don't have to be afraid to play outside. All these beautiful trees. Look at all these Christmas trees. I always wanted a real one at home! We did have a real one this Christmas in the convent."

"Next Christmas, Harlem, you can have your pick. Your grandpa will cut which ever tree you want down," Boone said.

"Grandpa! Grandpa!"

"Good mornin' Harlem. Did you eat your breakfast?"

"Yes sir, it was delicious. Mr. Boone is a real good cook. He's almost as good of a cook as my mama."

"Harlem, there's a place I want to show you a little further up the ridge here at the flat of the mountain. Come on. If you can't make it, I'll have to tote you on my back," Brady said.

I'm tough like you Grandpa. I'll make it."

"I don't doubt you one bit."

It was a climb, but Harlem made it to the top.

Harlem had never really been to a cemetery before, but she knew that this was just that, a cemetery. She looked at every handmade stone until she came to one that she recognized.

"Grandpa, this stone says David Brady O'Brannan. Is that my daddy?"

"Yes, it is Harlem. It most certainly is."

"He really is here?" Harlem asked Brady in disbelief.

"He's been here for almost nine years. Are you ok Harlem?"

"Grandpa, I feel all tingly inside to be this close to my daddy." Harlem sat on the bench that Brady usually sits on and got this huge smile on her face.

"Grandpa, would it be ok to bury my mother with him?"

Boone and Brady looked a little puzzled.

"Harlem, your mother is buried in New York, isn't she?"

"No, I have her ashes with me. Sister Delores told me the people at the mortuary were supposed to bury her in Potter's Field. That's a place where people go that can't afford a nice coffin and a nice place to be buried. Well, they lied. My mama got cremated instead and my good friend, Mr. Abermann, found her and gave the box of ashes to Sister

Mary Wagner

Delores to give to me. Sister Delores said I have to bury Mama in the ground as soon as I found a special place."

"Brady, what is she talkin' about? I'm all mixed up, cremated, ashes, all these people she's namin'."

"I'll explain it to you one day Brady. You found the special place Harlem. Right beside your daddy is where your mama belongs. There's just one problem. The ground is too frozen. We're goin' to have to wait until early spring. We can have a little ceremony and a picnic right here when we put her box in the ground. How about that? I don't have any type of tool that could break this ground up in this kind of weather. That way we can carve your mama's name on a stone. You can pick it out and help me carve it."

"I understand Grandpa and that is ok with me. I can pick a lot of pretty flowers then. Do you get a lot of pretty flowers around here in the spring?"

"Are you kiddin'. We have the most beautiful wildflowers that you will ever lay your eyes on. You're goin' to be able to pick blue violets, blue bells, periwinkles, day lilies, flaming azaleas and so many more. And the smell of the honeysuckle lingers here all spring and summer. Isn't that right Boone?"

"It sure is. In the spring and summer you're not goin' to believe how beautiful the mountain is. You think it's pretty now, wait until then," Boone said.

"I can't wait. I'm so happy here Grandpa!"

"You don't know how good those words make me feel Harlem. But Miss Sara was right you know. I'm goin' have to take you down the mountain to Kolter Elementary and enroll you in school, maybe even tomorrow."

"You don't understand. I love school. I love to study about things and I like to read a lot of books. I just hope the kids here like me in school."

Boone speaks up. "There ain't no way that somebody ain't goin' to like you. Put that worry on the bottom of your list."

"So if you're up to it, how about tomorrow mornin' goin' down to school and gettin' you enrolled? Then after we do that, you can go with me and Boone so I can make my delivery."

"Grandpa, you're saying words I want to hear!"

chapter 17

THE NEXT MORNING Harlem was quite nervous. She is in a town she knows nothing about, adjusting to her new home and Grandpa. She is also faced with starting a new school, with new teachers and new classmates.

"Grandpa, my stomach doesn't feel very good. I don't think I want any breakfast."

Brady felt Harlem's head and said, "don't feel hot, but I guess we can stop by old Doc Weller's then before we go to school. Maybe you got some kind of virus. He's got a needle for everything. He'll have you feelin' better in no time."

"No, no, it's really not that bad. I'll probably feel a lot better in a little while," Harlem said.

Brady knew Harlem was nervous, not scared, but so was he. He thought that if he showed her how nervous he was, she would feel better.

Brady looked at Harlem and said, "I don't know about you, but I am a bundle of nerves. I ain't been in a school house for years."

"Don't worry Grandpa. They won't make you go. You're too old."

"Well thanks a lot! That makes me feel a lot better. I knew I got old for a reason!"

"How many grades did you go to Grandpa?"

"Can't remember. Wasn't too many. Way back when I was young, most kids helped their folks on the farms. We used to have corn fields, cows, pigs, chickens and anything else we could raise and sell. Times were hard in those years. A couple of dollars bought a whole lot more than it does now. Yeah, times were hard. But we had our family all livin' here together, workin' the fields. The best part of the day was evenin' after supper. My gandpa would sit on the porch in the warmer weather or sit in front of the woodstove in the winter and tell stories about Ireland and what it was like for him as a boy. Grandma would laugh and make fun of him. Yeah, I miss those days."

"Maybe we can do that now. I can tell stories about St. Anthony's and the sisters and Officer Lopez and Mr. Abermann. You can tell me stories about my daddy. And we got Mr. Boone to tell us about the old days when Daniel Boone visited his family."

"You know, that is a good suggestion except the part about Boone. I'm afraid his stories will probably be a little far-fetched. What do you think?"

Harlem starts to laugh. "I think so too, but we shouldn't say anything to him. I don't want to hurt his feelings."

Brady got up to look out the window. He sent Boone to the barn to get the some tools for their delivery. "You couldn't hurt Boone if you threw a brick at his head," Brady said.

"Grandpa, I would never throw a brick at Mr. Boone's head."

"Little girl, you got to learn about jokin' around. I was just jokin' about that. Boone looks like he's ready to go. You feelin' any better? I want you to try and eat this apple on the way to school. You got to have somethin' on your stomach or I heard a person's mind don't work too good. I even got this sandwich wrapped special for lunch just in case you get to start school today."

"Ok, I'll eat the apple. But talking to you must have helped because I forgot all about my stomach ache," Harlem said.

"Well we better get goin' Harlem. I think school starts at eight o'clock."

"Be back later Blue Boy. Take care of Gladys, but don't eat her egg," Harlem said.

Kolter Elementary School really wasn't that far from Brady's home once you got off that winding mountain road. The other half of the building was the high school. The building was old and really needed a lot of renovations, but there was no money in the town budget.

Sara happened to be walking into the school when she saw Brady's truck pull into the parking lot. "Hi Brady. I see you and Boone must be showing Harlem all the sites in Kolter. Believe me, Harlem, don't blink, because you're going to miss a lot."

Boone looked at Sara. "We're just abidin' by what you said the other day."

Sara looking puzzled said, "what do you mean Boone?"

Brady answered that question, "you were right. We thought it only right and fair to Harlem to enroll her in school today. Do you think if we enroll her today, they will let her go to class today?"

Sara was really at a loss for words. Kolter was still a segregated school and town. Even though Harlem was very light skinned, she knew Principal Floyd Blackwater's hands would be tied even if he let her enroll. When Sara mentioned enrolling Harlem, she really thought Brady would have considered the colored school across from Mama Lucille's restaurant. Sara wasn't about to say anything to Brady. She didn't want to hurt his or Harlem's feelings. "What I can do is introduce you to our principal and go from there. Just follow me and I'll take you to his office."

Brady turned to Boone. "Boone, you wait out here. It shouldn't take too long. If it does, just come on in and ask for the principal's office."

"I sure am used to findin' the principal's office. I was in there most of the day way back when I went to school."

Everyone laughed.

Principal Blackwater was sitting behind his desk when Sara, Brady and Harlem walked in. "Mr. Blackwater, I would like you to meet Mr. Brady O'Brannan and his granddaughter, Harlem O'Brannan."

The principal got up to shake Brady's hand. "What can I do for you Mr. O'Brannan?"

"I came here today to enroll my granddaughter, Harlem in school."

Mr. Blackwater looked at Harlem and said to Brady. "I take it sir that this is the little girl you want to enroll here at our fine school today?"

"Yes sir, that's Harlem."

Mr. Blackwater looked at Sara and said, "Miss Mason would you take Harlem out of the room and let her sit right outside, then please come back into the office. Thank you."

Sara takes Harlem right outside of Mr. Blackwater's office then goes right back in.

Brady looked at Mr. Blackwater and said, "is there some kind of paper I have to sign so she can start school today?"

"Mr. O'Brannan, I'm afraid it's not that simple."

"Well then, if it's a lot of paperwork, I'll have to take them home and fill them out because I don't have my glasses with me. She can still start today can't she?"

"Mr. O'Brannan what race is Harlem?"

"What do you mean race?"

"Is she colored or is she white?"

"She's part of me. She's my granddaughter," Brady said.

"Mr. O'Brannan, no doubt she is part of you. But her race is part white and part colored. There are only two spaces on the enrollment form for race. One line is white and the other line is colored. Which line would you choose? How do you think I feel? Do you see any word under race that says American Indian? I am an Indian. What block would I check? So don't feel so agitated Mr. O'Brannan. My descendants were here before the colored or white settlers. If an Indian came in here to enroll their child, I would have to tell him that they have schools on the reservations. Do you think that is right?" Mr. Blackwater said.

Brady stood up and said, "I would choose, Mr. Blackwater, to erase both of those lines because neither one should be necessary in order to enroll a child in school that wants to learn."

"I don't have that option here and neither does any school in Kolter County that I know of. I didn't make the rules Mr. OBrannan. It is my job to see that they are followed. If I don't abide by the rules, the school board has the right to replace me on the spot."

Brady's face started to turn red. Sara could tell he was ready to explode and broke in the conversation. "Mr. Blackwater, what if we gave Harlem the State Assessment Test to see where she stands with her peers. If she tests well, she will only be an asset to our school. After all, we can argue that she is half white, living with Mr. O'Brannan, who is her grandfather, and pays taxes towards the school. Therefore, she should be allowed to enroll in this school."

"Mr. Blackwater, the only reason you ain't seen me walk out of that door is because this isn't about me or for me. This is for my granddaughter who has already lost two parents and doesn't need to be told she's not wanted here because she's not the right color. In the school where she came from, she was accepted. She told me she wants to be a doctor one day and by golly I'm goin' to do whatever it takes to make sure that she at least gets that chance."

Mr. Blackwater said, "I'll probably hear from the school board, but I'm willing to give her a chance. Miss Mason, can you start the test in a few minutes. I'll have somebody take over your classes while you oversee the test. I'll just have to deal with the repercussions of my decision later."

"Yes sir, thank you. Brady I know that you and Boone have an important delivery to make today and this test takes about four hours. Why don't you make your delivery and come back and pick up Harlem. If school is out before you get back, I'll take her home with me. Boone knows where I live. Is that ok with you?" Sara asked.

"Sara I appreciate your kindness and thank you Mr. Blackwater for giving Harlem a chance," Brady said.

"Miss Mason, would you please take Harlem into the vacant office at the end of the lobby and start testing her. Don't leave Mr. O'Brannan. I just will be a few more minutes. I'd like to have a word with you."

"Sure, I don't mind Mr. Blackwater. I appreciate you givin' Harlem this opportunity."

"Mr. O'Brannan, it's not that I don't want to give Harlem a chance, but because of the narrow-minded people who run this town, I don't have a choice in a lot of decisions. Doesn't my last name Blackwater ring a bell in your mind?"

"Yes, sir it does, but I didn't want to say anything in front of Sara. Your family used to live across the ridge from my family. My grandpa and your grandpa were best friends. I think they even became blood brothers when they were boys."

Mr. Blackwater said, "I don't remember much at all because my parents sent me up North to school. The white people of Kolter didn't want to deal with us Cherokee Indians, or should I say they didn't know how to accept us. Your family was the only family that showed my family respect and kindness. My family moved to the Blue Ridge Mountains of North Carolina, but I own the family home now. Who knows, maybe someday I'll move up there myself and we will be neighbors Mr. O'Brannan."

"We wondered where the family moved to. It would be nice to have neighbors again. How come you come back this way after all these years?"

Mr. Blackwater said, "I graduated from Harvard University with a Doctorate in Education. Believe it or not, I couldn't get a job in Connecticut or any other state up North, so I came back to good old Kolter with all my wonderful memories — I say that as a joke. The people of Kolter are lucky. I have some of the best teachers right here. All of these teachers have their Bachelor Degrees and the few that don't are attending West Virginia University part time. The good people of Kolter don't realize they have a real, red-blooded Cherokee Indian as their principal. They needed somebody with credentials, and I had what they wanted. What I'm trying to say is, I actually know what a battle Harlem is going through and will go through, but I do feel she deserves the same rights as the other children here. Harlem is half white, but there are very few people in this town with an open mind. All they see is the brown in her skin."

"Mr. Blackwater, I am really grateful to you. If you ever need me for anything, you just drop by any time. You know where I live."

"I thank you Mr. O'Brannan. Can I call you Brady?"

"Sure, but I'll still call you Mr. Blackwater, maybe Floyd when nobody is around."

They shake hands.

"We probably won't find out until the end of the week what the test results are. I guess you better make that delivery Mr. . . . , I mean Brady."

Brady and Boone got into the truck and headed for an area outside of McSchowell County to make their delivery by noon.

chapter 18

THE TRUCK WAS packed solid with heavy lumber for a new customer of Brady's. An outsider named Henry Thomas signed the order for the lumber a few months before. This was about the fifth delivery of lumber to that area. Brady really didn't know Mr. Thomas that well but it was a big order and financially got Boone and Brady through those hard winter months. Mr. Thomas also put half the money up front and the rest at this last delivery. Brady never had a good-paying customer like Mr. Thomas before. He still had customers that still owed him money from years ago. But Brady being Brady and a soft touch never hounded any of his customers for the balance of their money.

When Brady and Boone pulled up in the truck, they noticed a well-dressed man alongside of Mr. Thomas along with three children. They had no idea who they were. The area where the lumber was to be dropped off was in a beautiful valley surrounded by tall oak trees and a small stream running through it. Brady couldn't help but to think that it reminded him of his own beautiful mountaintop.

Mr. Thomas and the stranger, along with the three children, walked over to meet Brady and Boone. "Brady and Boone, I'd like to introduce you to the owner of this place, Mr. Maurice Duval."

Brady shook hands with Mr. Duval first. "Nice to meet you Mr. Duval. This is my partner Boone."

Boone shakes Mr. Duval's hand. "Same here Mr. Duval. Are these your kids?"

"Yes, they are. Come over here and meet Mr. Brady and Mr. Boone."

The children, two boys and a girl really didn't want to say hello but their father insisted.

"This is Louis, my oldest son. He's twelve. This is Lillian, my daughter. She will be nine in another month. And the little one over there is Matthew who just turned five."

Boone said to the children, "pleasure to meet your acquaintance."

Brady then said, "nice to meet you all."

The oldest boy laughed and said to his sister. "Did you hear that? You all."

Brady didn't want to be rude and say anything back to the boy. He just looked at Boone and said, "we got to go Boone. It's gettin' late and we got to pick Harlem up from school."

Boone just stared at the boy and said, "yeah, Brady, the best thing we can do right now is leave."

Just then Mr. Duval interrupted them and said, "are you talking about the school in Kolter?"

Brady said, "yes sir, I am."

Mr. Duval said, "I'll probably be enrolling my children in school there."

Boone spoke up and said, "ain't McSchowell a little closer?"

"Yes, it is closer, but the educational system in my view is very substandard. I heard Kolter offers more in their curriculum," Mr. Duval said.

Brady looks at Mr. Duval and says, "we got to go. Thanks for your business."

While driving back to Kolter, Boone couldn't stop talking about how rude Mr. Duval's children were. "He didn't even correct that boy when he laughed and mocked us. And the only reason he ain't puttin' those kids in McSchowell county schools is probably 'cause they got kicked out – substandard my foot. I'm darn sure that boy he called Louis got the boot, maybe not the girl or the little kid, not yet anyway. If that boy was mine, I'd wash his mouth out, then I'd put him outside in this cold bustin' up wood."

"This world is made up of all kinds of people Boone. That boy's got to grow up someday too. I'm sure there is goin' to be somebody out there just like him that will give it right back to him. That's when he'll know he's a man not a boy anymore."

"I hope that time comes his way real soon, Brady."

"Boone, I've heard that name, Duval, before but I can't place it. Have you heard that name?"

"You're right Brady. Seems I've even seen it somewhere, but for the life of me, I can't remember where."

"Maybe it will hit us in the head and we'll remember. Right now I'm hopin' Harlem isn't nervous takin' that test," Brady said.

"Brady, she's a smart little girl. Don't you worry any about her. She'll do fine."

Brady and Boone made it back to school just in time. Harlem just finished her test. Sara walked out with Harlem and said, "she did fine Brady, but we won't know how she scored for a few days. She deserves a treat for sitting through four hours of non-stop testing. Right Harlem?"

"Right Miss Sara; that is if Grandpa and Mr. Boone think I do."

Brady looks at Harlem. "Of course we think you deserve it. Hop in and we'll stop by Mama Lucille's restaurant and get us some of her homemade ice cream. Sara would you like to come along or do you have to get back to class?"

"Brady, I appreciate it. But you're right. I have to get back to class. Mr. Blackwater was nice enough to have somebody take over my class, but I do have to get back."

Brady and Sara gazed at each other for a few seconds then Brady said, "we can all get us some ice cream another day Sara, if that's ok with you."

"I'll keep you at your word Brady. Boone knows where I live," Sara said.

Brady said, "so do I Sara. Thanks again for everything you did for Harlem."

Everyone says their good-byes and Brady drives over to Mama Lucille's restaurant for some good homemade ice cream.

As they got out of the truck at Mama Lucille's, Brady noticed a sheet of yellow paper lying on the ground. He picked it up thinking it was some kind of advertisement. After they went into the restaurant and sat down, he gave the paper to Boone and said, "Boone, I don't have my glasses, looks like an advertisement, what does it say?"

Boone took the paper and glanced at it and said, "I knew it, I knew it."

Harlem said, "what did you know Mr. Boone?"

"Brady, remember we said we heard that name, "Duval", before?"

"Yeah, so what are you tryin' to say Boone?"

"Harlem, how about you goin' up and orderin' us three big vanilla cones and here's a nickel for the juke box. Just pick out what song you like."

"Ok Mr. Boone, I get it, you want to talk to my grandpa in private. Can I order a little ice cream cup for Blue Boy?"

Brady laughed and said, "Blue Boy has got a good life. Just get him a small cup Harlem."

Harlem goes over to the counter to order ice cream.

"I told you Brady, she's smart as a whip."

"Boone, what's does that paper say?" Brady asked.

"It says that this here fella' we met today, Mr. Maurice Duval, is the owner of Duval Mountaintop Minin' Company out of Canada. It says here that he is offerin' top dollar for homes and land, especially mountain land here in Kolter. He's comin' to Kolter next month and he's goin' to give a talk in the Town Hall buildin'."

"I hope these people 'round these parts are smart enough, Boone, not to sell any of their property to him. All they got to do is drive to McSchowell County and see the mess they made strip minin' for coal. But a lot of farms are failin' around here plus there's not much work in Kolter anymore. I'm afraid his money won't let the people here think straight. I wish I knew months ago about Duval, I never would have sold any lumber to him. I signed a contract and that's as bindin' as a man's word. After he bought all that land up for hardly nothin' in McSchowell, then tore it to pieces, he's got the nerve to build him a fine house in that big valley with the profit he made from poor folks," Brady said.

"Brady, Duval is a snake. That's why he had that guy, Thomas, deal with us. He figured if we knew who he was, we wouldn't sell any lumber to him. Seein' how there ain't anybody but us cuttin' timber and sellin' it around these parts, maybe he would have high-tailed it back to Canada if we told him we weren't goin' to deal with him," Boone said.

"There are a couple of good things Boone. One is, I own a good part of Kolter Mountain and Mr. Blackwater, the principal, owns the rest.

I know I'm not sellin' and I hope he never does. A lot of the Blackwater family moved to the Blue Ridge Mountains of North Carolina. Once the Blackwater family finds out I'm keepin' my land, I'm sure they will encourage Mr. Blackwater not to sell. Now these farmers on the lower mountain ridges might consider sellin' to him, but I hope I can talk them out of it. Here comes Miss Lucille and Harlem with our ice cream. We'll talk later."

Mama Lucille notices that Boone has the yellow paper lying on the table and said, "two guys came in here today and wanted to put a bunch of those papers in here for people to read. I told them if they didn't get out of here and take their papers with them, that I was gettin' my rifle out and I would target practice on them. They couldn't run out fast enough. Guess I lost two new customers. Was worth it though – the look on their faces. I've been to these towns after they do their business. It is just pitiful, plum pitiful the way they leave it and promise to come back and fix it and you don't see hide or hair of them anymore. And all that noise and dust and dirt from that dynamite, makes the people start sellin' their houses. When they move, people like me go out of business, and where in the world am I goin' to go?"

Boone laughed and said, "you did the right thing Miss Lucille. Hopefully everybody else in town knows that mountaintop mining is no good for a town, especially a pretty mountain town like Kolter."

"Well they won't be back here anymore. Now you all eat your ice cream and enjoy it."

Harlem remarks, "we sure will Miss Lucille."

Brady knew in his heart, the problem with the Duval Mining Company was going to become a fight he didn't need at this time in his life.

chapter 19

ABOUT A WEEK passed after Harlem took her test. Sara got word to Boone to tell Brady and Harlem to come into town and stop by the school. "Boone, you're going to have to convince Brady to get a telephone. I'm kind of scared to drive up that mountain of his. If you didn't stop by and see my daddy once in a while, he never would have gotten this message."

"Sara, you know how Brady is. He kind of keeps to himself, but you're absolutely right. He has a granddaughter now and he's got more responsibility and he should have a telephone. I'm goin' to talk to him about it. Can you tell me if Harlem did ok on that there test?"

"Boone, I'm not allowed to say. Why don't you come with Brady to school? Tell him to come around nine o'clock."

"I'll do just that Sara. You know spring is right around the corner. Think you'll be goin' to the spring dance at Town Hall?"

"I'm pretty sure I'll go. Do you think Brady will be there?"

"I know he will when he finds out you're comin'." I better get my hind end on up that mountain and let him know about goin' to school tomorrow. See you Sara."

"Bye Boone and thanks."

Boone pulls his truck into Brady's yard and hears a lot of hammering going on. "What the blazes is he buildin' now?"

Just then Harlem runs out to the truck to meet Boone. "Mr. Boone, Mr. Boone, come and see what Grandpa is making for me."

"What in tarnation is that? You already got that old outhouse over yonder. Why you buildin' another one?"

Blue boy is jumping all over Boone "I love you too boy. I got this treat for you – sit. Good boy."

"Boone, this ain't no outhouse. This is a chicken coop. Mrs. Corby is gettin' rid of twenty of her layin' hens. She's given them to Harlem."

"Isn't that great Mr. Boone. I am going to sell the eggs. This way Gladys will have some new friends and I can make some money."

"Harlem, Gladys just ain't the socializin' type with other chickens. She likes people not chickens."

"Oh, she'll get used to it Boone. What brings you up here?" Brady asked.

"Brady, you're goin' to have to get a telephone up here. I ran into Sara and she said you and Harlem need to be at school tomorrow at nine o'clock. She wanted to come up here herself but was afraid to drive."

"I hope it's good news. Harlem's been out of school too long. And I really was thinkin' of gettin' a telephone since Harlem is livin' here now. I might not be here and she may need to call somebody or have an emergency and call the sheriff."

"That useless man in town we call sheriff. You should run for sheriff, Brady."

"I'm too old and too tired and I ain't leavin' this mountain to live in town."

Harlem looks at both of them. "I know somebody from New York that would make a good sheriff. He knows all the laws and everything."

"I bet I know his name. You talk about him all the time Harlem. Is it Officer Lopez?" Brady said.

"Grandpa, how did you guess?"

"I heard a lot of good things about him Harlem, but I really don't think he would leave New York to come to this tiny mountain town. Anyway you told me he wrote and told you he made detective."

"He did. He is a detective now. He said maybe one day Sister Delores and him will visit me. Do you care Grandpa if they do?" Harlem asked.

"Harlem, I'd be happy to meet these people. They were good to you and looked out for you and that's all I care about."

"Let's go in and get some supper. Boone you're stayin' I hope," Brady said.

"Did you ever know me to turn down a meal?" Boone asked.

The next morning Brady, Boone and Harlem drove to Kolter Elementary to meet up with Sara for a meeting with Mr. Blackwater to see if Harlem passed or failed the State Assessment Test.

Boone sat in the outer office while Brady and Harlem went into Mr. Blackwater's office with Sara.

Mr. Blackwater said, "Sara, would you please tell us how Harlem did on the test."

Harlem was very nervous and Brady could see that. He whispered in her ear. "Whatever happens here, you're the smartest little girl I ever met." Harlem gave him a little smile.

Sara started her assessment. "I not only checked Harlem's test, but it was verified by Mrs. Lydia Pruitt, sixth grade history teacher and Mr. Russell Kirby, our sixth grade math teacher. Harlem excelled in every test, especially reading, math, and science. Her total average score for all subjects including spelling, history and English was ninety-eight percent. Never in the history of Kolter Elementary was that ever achieved. As of now Harlem is in the third grade but is capable of working at a sixth grade level. It is my opinion that Harlem skips the fourth and fifth grades and be put in a sixth grade class with your approval, Mr. Blackwater and with Mr. O'Brannan's approval."

There was complete silence. Harlem looked at Brady and smiled and he looked at her, put his arms around her and said, "I am so proud of you. Looks like that dream you have of becomin' a doctor one day is really goin' to happen."

Harlem looked at Mr. Blackwater and said, "does all that mean I get to go to this school?"

Everybody laughed.

Mr. Blackwater said, "Harlem, you can start tomorrow. I am a little leery about letting you jump two grades. I need to talk further with Miss Mason. I am a little concerned about the social impact. By that I mean sixth graders are somewhat taller than you Harlem and I don't want to see you get picked on. What do you think Miss Mason?"

Sara said, "I understand how you feel Mr. Blackwater. What if we tried her out in the fifth grade first? If she has no problems socially or academically, we can leave her there until the end of the year."

Sara looks at Brady. "It's up to you also Brady. Would you like us to put her in the fifth grade and see how everything works out?"

Brady throws the question to Harlem. "What do you say Harlem? It is really up to you."

Harlem looked around the room at everyone and said, "I'll try the fifth grade. I miss being in school. I want to start tomorrow."

Mr. Blackwater puts his hand out and shakes Harlem's hand. "It's a deal Harlem, and a very big pleasure to have you. Report tomorrow morning, at eight o'clock, to room ten. Your teacher will be Mrs. Julie Hollins."

Harlem went into the outer office to tell Boone that she not only passed the test but she is skipping the rest of the third grade and all of the fourth.

"What did I tell you Brady? I told you she was smart. I'm so proud of you too. I feel like I just passed that test." Boone hugged Harlem; they both went out and got in the truck.

On the way out the door Sara told Brady he was so lucky to have Harlem, not because she was so intelligent, but because she was respectful and kind hearted. "She had a good upbringing Brady. Her mother did everything right in raising her."

"I never met her mother, Sara, but she must have been sent down here by angels to raise such a good, sweet girl. I wish now I was there while she was growin' up, but New York is pretty far from Kolter, West Virginia."

"Brady, Boone mentioned to me that you might go to the spring dance in a few weeks."

"Boone mentions a lot of things. Sara, if I do go, would you like to go with me?"

"I most certainly will Brady. You just let me know for sure. Harlem can be our chaperone."

They both laugh.

chapter 20

THE NEXT MORNING Harlem was ready and eager to start her new school. She wasn't nervous at all. She was excited. She was even going to get to ride on the school bus like Arlene and Joseph, her two good friends from St. Anthony's school, did. She wanted to walk down the mountain to Brady's mailbox where the school bus was to pick her up, but Brady drove her down. They both sat in the truck waiting for the school bus. Of course Blue Boy sat in the middle of the seat.

"Grandpa, you didn't have to drive me down here. I've walked down here before. You and Mr. Boone have got a lot of timber to cut."

"That's ok Harlem. There may come a time when I can't drive you down here. I'll be here after school too. The bears are comin' out from hibernatin' all winter. I feel better lettin' you sit in the truck until the bus comes."

"Grandpa, remember what you said about burying my mama with my daddy? Do you think the ground will be a little softer by April 1st?"

"We'll have to wait and see Harlem. What is so important about April 1st?"

"It's my mother's birthday."

Harlem's eyes start to water. "That was going to be my birthday present to her."

Brady pulled one of her pigtails and said, "just for you, I'm goin' to make that ground extra soft that day. Now stop worrin' about stuff and think about how much fun you're goin' to have today. And here comes the bus."

The bus was only half full. There were other stops to make that morning to pick up more children. When Harlem got off the bus she went straight to Room 10, Mrs. Hollins fifth grade class.

When Harlem walked in the classroom, everyone stared at her. Mrs. Hollins introduced Harlem as the new girl. She sat beside a girl named Velma Little. Velma looked at Harlem shyly and said, "hi, my name is Velma."

Harlem also introduced herself. "My name is Harlem."

Harlem couldn't help notice that Velma was quite a big girl. She reminded Harlem of a chunky little girl at St. Anthony's that the kids would make fun of and call "fatso". Her name was Myra. Myra always had a nice, neat uniform on every day. Harlem noticed Velma's unkempt hair and her worn and faded dress. But Velma was clean and so were her clothes.

Lunchtime came. Harlem couldn't wait to eat her sandwich. It was a piece of Sunday's chicken between two pieces of homemade bread that Boone made. She glanced over at Velma's lunch and she had a piece of cornbread. It wasn't even wrapped; it was just thrown in an old bag with a couple of crackers. Milk was free, donated by one of the farmers who raised cows.

"Velma, would you like half of my sandwich?" Harlem asked.

"No thank you Harlem. I got plenty here. Harlem can I touch your hair?"

"Why? Go ahead."

Velma touched her hair and said, "your hair is so soft. Everybody says colored people's hair is supposed to feel like wire, but your hair don't feel that way at all."

Harlem was kind of hurt but she expected these kinds of questions. After all, she was the only person of color in the whole school.

"My hair is like my daddy's and so are my eyes. My skin is like my mama's."

"I see now. I bet your daddy has pretty hair and pretty blue eyes like you. You're lucky Harlem, you are pretty. I bet nobody makes fun of you," Velma said.

"My parents are both up in Heaven now. I live with my grandfather." Harlem said sadly.

"I'm sorry Harlem that you don't have any parents, but at least you have a grandfather to take care of you."

"I really love Grandpa and I know he wouldn't let anybody make fun of me."

"These kids call me fatty, chubby, ugly. They make fun of my hair and tell me I have cooties and that I'm dirty. I try not to cry in front of them but sometimes it is hard to hold my tears in," Velma said.

"I don't think you are any of those names. You just ignore those kids."

"It's not that easy. It hurts me inside. My daddy can't work and my mama does laundry for people. We don't have a lot of money to buy stuff with."

Just then the bell rang for lunch to be over and class to start again.

Harlem realized, after her conversation with Velma, how lucky she was to have had a mother that worked hard and believed in getting a good education in order to get ahead in life. She felt she was still lucky to have her grandpa in her life now to fulfill her dream of having a family like other kids had.

When Harlem got off the school bus, she saw Grandpa building a little shed beside the mailbox at the foot of the mountain where the bus picks her up. Blue Boy ran up to meet Harlem.

"Grandpa, what's that for? Good boy, Blue, did you miss me?"

"Well I thought about things, and I figured there might be a time when you can't sit here in my truck. I thought if it is bad weather, Harlem is goin' to have to stand in rain or snow waitin' for the bus. So I built you a little bus stop shed."

"Thank you Grandpa. You are so smart to think of everything."

"Oh, and by the way, remember I told you I was buildin' an extra room for a lady named Mrs. Higgins. She lives on that small mountain called Stoneface. Well, I told her you were in the egg rasin' business and she would like two dozen a week. Then I stopped by Mama Lucille's restaurant, dropped a few words about the chickens and she wants all the rest you can give her. You think I'm a smart businessman?"

"You sure are Grandpa. You think fifty-cents a dozen is fair?" Harlem asked.

"Sure is. Tyler's Grocery Market charges sixty-five cents and they are those idy-biddy eggs – ain't worth more than a quarter a dozen.

You got them big old Rhode Island Red brown eggs. You're in business now girl. Somethin' botherin' you Harlem? You look like your mind is someplace else."

"Mrs. Hollins sat me beside this girl named Velma Little. I noticed she didn't have much for lunch. Then today on the playground the kids called her all kinds of names — fatso, bullfrog, pig — really nasty stuff. She said her daddy is sick and her mama takes in laundry and they don't have much money. Why do kids do that?"

Brady said, "They do that because they weren't lucky enough to be taught respect for others when they were little tykes. Your mama taught you right. Me and your Grandma Kathleen taught your daddy respect. If it doesn't start at home, you ain't goin' to get it anywhere else. Now I know Mr. Little, Velma's daddy. I think I'm goin' to pay him a visit. I do believe his sickness can be cured. There's a job sweepin' at Mama Lucille's restaurant. Think I'll tell him about it tomorrow. Ain't right his little girl is hungry. I'll take care of that situation tomorrow Harlem. Well look who's comin' for a visit. Come on in Boone. You're just in time to cook us some supper."

They all laugh.

After supper Brady told Boone about Velma's father while Harlem was in another room doing her homework.

Boone said, "you talkin' about that old drunk Coot Little? Why he ain't sick Brady. He's a plum drunk every time I see him. Reason that little girl does without is because he takes his wife's pay and stays drunk all week. He needs a knock on the side of his head and a job."

"You know that and so do I, but nobody else needs to know. It's about time Coot became a family man. I aim on makin' him one tomorrow," Brady replied.

The next day after Harlem went to school, Brady rode down the holler to a run-down house where the Little family lived. He knocked on the door and got no answer. "Coot Little. You in there. It's Brady, Brady O'Brannan. I need to talk to you. If you don't come out, I'm comin' in."

"Ok, ok, I'm comin.' What do you want?" Coot said.

Brady went in, took the whisky bottle on the table and poured it down the sink. He went around the room, found more and did the same thing.

"Get out of my house or I'm goin' to shoooot you between the eyeballs," Coot said, holding his rifle. He couldn't even stand up straight, he was so drunk.

Brady took his rifle away and said, "sit down before I knock you down. There's somethin' you got to know. You got a little girl in school that don't have decent clothes or even a decent lunch to eat. She is ashamed Coot, ashamed in front of the other kids. And all they do is make fun of her. You're the one should be ashamed and made fun of not her. You didn't know none of that did you. You had your last drink today. There's a job at Mama Lucille's restaurant, pays $2.00 an hour. I talked to her already and the job is yours. But you better not mess up, or I'll be back here. I swear I will. You take that pay and buy your little girl a few nice dresses and make sure she has a nice lunch. And If I find out you spent one dime of your pay or your wife's pay on drinkin', your carcass is mine, and believe me, you don't want that to happen. Now get dressed we're goin' into town to get that job."

"I swear Brady, I didn't know none of that. That's my sweet baby girl. I'm goin' to try and do what is best for my family. Nobody ever offered me any help. I'm beholdin' to you Brady."

"Let's get goin'. I got a lot of work I got to get done today, Coot."

chapter 21

IT WAS ALMOST the end of March and Harlem knew that meant that spring was on the way, the ground would be softer and she would be able to rightfully bury her mother next to her father. Everything seemed to be turning around for the best. Harlem noticed Velma had a few newer dresses she was wearing to school and a nice lunch every day, and she saw a little bit of a change in Velma. Velma was more confident and proud of her father since he got his new job at Mama Lucille's. And Coot, of all people, never took another drop of whisky. He was the best worker Mama Lucille ever hired. Harlem's egg business was even thriving. She was able to buy more hens for laying and had more customers to deliver eggs to. Brady was never happier. He knew Harlem was absolutely happy and contented and he finally got the nerve up a few weeks before to ask Sara to the spring dance.

What's the old saying? "Behind every cloud there is a silver lining". Well "behind a silver lining there is a cloud". The "cloud" is the Duval family. Mr. Duval came into town to enroll his son Louis and his daughter Lillian in Kolter Elementary. Matthew wasn't ready for first grade yet and the school had no kindergarten.

Sara had to test both of the Duval children just as she tests every child that is new to the school.

Mr. Duval was distraught over the enrollment process and didn't think his children should be submitted to any of these tests. He walked right into the principal's office and demanded to talk to him. He said, "Mr. Backwater, I don't believe and do not want my children to be subjected to being placed according to their test results. They both excelled academically in the private schools they were in, in New Hampshire. My son should finish out the sixth grade and my daughter should finish out the third grade."

"But Mr. Duval, what if they test very high? We can move them up a grade or put them in a more advanced curriculum. That is the purpose of the testing. We don't want our children to be held back intellectually. You wouldn't want that would you?" Mr. Blackwater asked.

"I really never thought of it that way. I'm sure you will be surprised how knowledgeable they both are. I just hope this tiny school is equipped to give them the highest level of teaching possible," Mr. Duval said.

Mr. Blackwater said, "I wouldn't worry about that Mr. Duval. We will let you know the results as soon as we evaluate the scores. Nice meeting you."

"Blackwater, isn't that an Indian name. Did you get your degree on the reservation Mr. Blackwater?" Mr. Duval asked in a condescending voice.

"If you want to call Harvard University in Connecticut a reservation, that's up to you. Good day Mr. Duval," Mr. Blackwater said.

On the way out of school, Mr. Duval noticed Harlem coming out of the girl's restroom and going back into class. He marched himself back into the principal's office.

"Mr. Blackwater, are you integrated at this school? This is one of the last towns I would think would be integrated. I just saw a colored girl in the hallway."

"Mr. Blackwater just stared at him and said, "what is your point, Mr. Duval?"

"I thought it odd in this part of the country to see a colored person in an all-white school this soon."

"Mr. Duval, this little girl is also white. She is also the brightest student in the whole school and she is an asset to Kolter Elementary and will be one day to Kolter High School."

"I get it now; you understand where she is coming from. You're one hundred percent red, she's half white and half brown. I guess you both understand each other more," Mr. Duval said.

"Mr. Duval, please step out of my office, NOW!!!!"

"Don't forget Mr. Blackwater, make sure you call me when you get the test results."

Mr. Blackwater was beside himself. Hopefully this man wasn't going to start trouble for him or Harlem. He didn't know it but Sara was in the next room. The door was open and she heard everything.

"Mr. Blackwater, I heard everything he said to you and I don't believe what I heard. I'm sorry."

"Miss Mason, he is just a bigot in a well-dressed suit. Hopefully, he won't cause any trouble at this school. I think it best you don't say anything to Mr. O'Brannan about what transpired here."

"I would never reiterate to anyone the private conversations that go on in this office Mr. Blackwater," Sara said.

"I know you wouldn't Miss Mason. I know you wouldn't," Mr. Blackwater said.

Kolter Elementary and the high school did not have a regular physical education teacher. Mr. Cornish, fourth grade teacher, usually took the students outside to play or on bad days the auditorium was used as a gym. Most of the time, the children did exercises, ran around or played volleyball.

A new teacher from New York started that Monday as the physical education instructor for the elementary students and high school students. His name was Mr. Roy Finch. He must have been in his early fifties. He had a rough complexion. He was tall and his chest and upper body was extremely large. He had grayish hair with a tint of brown and a big gray mustache. He spoke loud as if no one could hear him. Mr. Finch was a figure that scared most of the children, especially the younger ones. Mr. Blackwater had no choice. He was directed to hire a certified physical education teacher or one with a degree.

May was almost two months away. The school was going to celebrate May Day that year. The students would dance around the maypole, crown a king and queen, and each grade would be doing a skit for spring or a dance. The fifth grade, Harlem's class, would be learning to square dance.

It was up to Mr. Finch to teach each grade the skit or dance they were to do. Since it was still a little cold outside, activities relating to physical education were taught in the auditorium.

As the class walked into the auditorium, they got a good look at the new physical education teacher, Mr. Finch. There wasn't a sound to be heard as they gathered around and he introduced himself. You could see the hint of panic as he told the class what he expected out of them in his loud scratchy voice.

"My name is Mr. Finch. When you walk into this auditorium or outside on the playground in good weather, I don't expect to hear one sound out of any of you. If I do, you will go straight to the office and you will have detention after school. I expect a single file. I expect "Yes Sir" and "No Sir" coming from your lips. And you boy's, listen up, no horseplay. I'm not Mr. Cornish. I heard this was more of a play period. Well it's not anymore. The fifth grade is going to learn square dancing for May Day this year. I am going to show you a few of the calls and steps. So everybody grab a partner. I want to see a boy with a girl."

There were more girls than boys in the class. The only two without a partner were Velma and Harlem.

Mr. Finch stood staring at Velma and Harlem. His eyes looked as though he could have thrown darts out of them. "Hey, what are you two just going to stand there like two dummies? Get over here."

The two girls walked across the floor over to Mr. Finch. You couldn't hear a pin drop in the auditorium.

Mr. Finch pointed to Velma. "Get over here Tiny." The kids laughed while Velma held back tears.

Mr. Finch then pointed to Harlem. "You, I'm talking to you Sambo. Get over here. You two be partners with each other.

Harlem walked over to Mr. Finch, looked up at him and said, "my name is Harlem."

Everything was quiet again.

Mr. Finch looked down at Harlem and said, "what did you just say to me?"

"I said, Mr. Finch, my name is Harlem, not Sambo. And Velma's name is Velma not Tiny."

"Apparently, HARLEM, you didn't listen when I said I didn't want to hear a sound from anyone. You and VELMA can march yourselves down to the principal's office and sign the book for detention tonight," Mr. Finch said in his loud, nasty voice.

"But all I did was tell you what our names were," Harlem said.

"Get out of my sight now. And you both sign the book for two days!!" Mr. Finch hollered.

Velma and Harlem started down the hallway to the principal's office to sign the book.

Velma looked at Harlem with tears streaming down her face. "Why did you have to say anything? I'm used to being called names. Now the kids will make fun of me more and Mr. Finch will pick on me all the time now."

Harlem looked at her puzzled. "Do you think it was right that he called us names? He is a rude man. I don't want those kids to call me Sambo now. I thought we were friends and friends take up for each other."

"You got me into trouble Harlem. We're not friends anymore."

Harlem couldn't believe what Velma said. Velma hurt her with those words more than the words Mr. Finch used.

They both served detention after their last class. Sara happened to walk past the classroom and saw Harlem sitting there. Velma wouldn't sit next to her. She sat on the other side of the room.

"Harlem, surely you don't have detention."

"Yes, I do Miss Mason, so does Velma — all because of me."

"What happened?" Sara asked.

Harlem told Sara what Mr. Finch said to her and Velma. Sara was outraged. "That kind of name calling was uncalled for! I'm going to let Mr. Blackwater know what happened."

"Please don't Miss Mason. It will make things worse. I shouldn't have said anything. Now Velma doesn't want to be my friend anymore," Harlem said.

"Velma shouldn't feel that way. You took up for her. She should be glad she has a friend like you," Sara said.

"Please Miss Mason, don't tell Grandpa either. He'll be disappointed in me. I wish I never would have said anything." Harlem starts to cry.

"Harlem, you did the right thing. You and Velma are going to miss the bus. I'll take you both home," Sara said.

"Thanks Miss Mason, because Grandpa is going to be worried. Please don't tell him what happened," Harlem said.

"I won't say anything this time Harlem. But by not telling on Mr. Finch, he will probably do this to the other children because he'll think he got away with it the first time. If he does do this again, I want to know because I will inform Mr. Blackwater about his conduct," Sara said.

Brady was worried. He and Blue Boy were sitting in the truck waiting for Harlem when Sara pulled up and let her out. Sara already took Velma home and also had a talk with her outside of her car so Harlem couldn't hear.

Brady got out of the truck. "Harlem, I've been worried about you, what happened?"

Harlem looked up at Sara then her grandpa. "The bus had a flat tire and we had to wait for it to get fixed. Sorry Grandpa, I didn't have any way to let you know."

"That does it. Now I know tomorrow I'm goin' into town to the Telephone Office and puttin' in for a new phone. Takes somethin' like this to shake you up a little. Thank you Sara for bringin' Harlem home."

"Any time Brady. Now don't you forget about that spring dance next Saturday. And when you get that new phone number, make sure you give it to Harlem so the school will have it on their record."

"Don't worry, I'll do just that."

"Let's go up to the house Harlem. I've got supper made. You sure you're ok? You look a little down."

"I'm just hungry Grandpa that's all."

chapter 22

THE NEXT DAY at school Sara told Mr. Blackwater that the results for from the assessment test were in, and that Mr. Blackwater's secretary should call and have Mr. Duval and his two children come to the office so Sara could go over the results.

Mr. Duval, his son Louis and daughter Lillian, came into school that afternoon. They were invited into Mr. Blackwater's office to hear the results of the test from Sara.

Sara talked about Lillian's assessment first. "Lillian is working at the high end of the third grade. She passed all tests including math, reading, spelling, English, history and science exceptionally well. I recommend that she finish the third grade this year. I have a special group of children that she will be working with that have excelled in all third grade courses. I work with this group in preparing them to have a head start in the fourth grade. The fourth grade teacher will work with them individually to evaluate each student and determine how to adjust their academic curriculum. How does that sound to you Lillian?"

Lillian smiled and started to answer Sara. "That sounds ..."

Mr. Duval cut in the conversation. "I'm sure before the end of this year, Miss Mason, you will already know that Lillian will be moving onto the fifth grade and skipping the fourth."

"Mr. Duval, that is something I can't predict. I will watch Lillian's progression and get back to you by the end of the year," Sara said.

"Now let's find out the test results for my Louis. He did so well last year in Brookside Academy in New Hampshire, I'm sure he had no trouble with the assessment for this little mountain town school."

"Mr. Duval, this assessment test is generally the same in every state. I've seen several from other Northern states and there are very little differences," Sara said.

"Miss Mason, the key word you mentioned –"general". The school Louis attended was not general in any way. Academically, it was one of the best schools."

Sara looked at Mr. Duval. "Maybe Lillian would like to sit in the outer office while I go over Louis' assessment with you."

"No, No, that won't be necessary. Just sit there Lillian," Mr. Duval said.

"I know grade wise Louis is in the fifth grade and should be going into the sixth grade next September. Louis did not do well on any of the tests. I recommend that he finish the fifth grade this year and repeat the fifth grade again next year unless a lot of improvement is shown in the next three months before school is out for summer. If not, he can take classes this summer and he may be able to do well in the sixth, if the school determines that that is where he belongs next September."

"Father, she's crazy if she thinks I'm repeating the fifth grade or going to school all summer. I'll move back to New Hampshire with Mother. This school stinks," Louis said.

Mr. Blackwater spoke up and said, "we don't speak out disrespectfully in this school Louis. Miss Mason is more than qualified in determining the placement of students here at Kolter."

"You don't tell my son what he can say and what he can't say. I'll correct my children, not you, not some wild red-skin Indian that the town of Kolter ignorantly put in charge," Mr. Duval said.

Mr. Blackwater said, "that remark was uncalled for, but I won't take it out on your children. You either abide by the results of the test or you're free to take your children to another school."

Louis looked at his father and said, "I'm not repeating the fifth grade for nobody."

"Son, go out into the office. I'll straighten this out. And take your sister," Mr. Duval said.

Louis and Lillian exited the room.

Mr. Duval pounds his fist on Mr. Blackwater's desk. "My son will not repeat the fifth grade. Is that clear?"

Mr. Blackwater said, "If Miss Mason doesn't feel at the end of the year that he is ready for the sixth grade academically, he will repeat the fifth grade."

"I'll hire a scholar to home school him before I allow him to be embarrassed by failing," Mr. Duval said.

Sara said, "Mr. Duval, to be quite frank with you, I didn't want to hurt your son's feelings while he was in here. His test results were the worst I have ever seen. The results showed that Louis should be put back in the fourth grade. If he weren't so tall, I would recommend that you do just that. I'm afraid it would bring down his self-esteem if he were put back in the fourth grade at this time. Do you have any records with you from Brookside showing how Louis did in school? Some private schools, in order to keep their high standing will intentionally move a student forward that should be held back."

"Why I never, neither one of my children will be coming to this hick, low class mountain school. They will both be home schooled by a scholar of my choosing from one of the best Northern schools. You two should be ashamed. You let a little low-class colored girl go to school here and allow her to skip a grade. What's the reason for that? So that you can push integration down everybody's throat," Mr. Duval said.

Sara was beyond words. "That little girl got the highest scores ever, not only in this little hick town- mountain school, but every school in the whole state of West Virginia and she has an IQ of 160, which is the standard for a genius."

"That's ok. Before summer is out, I'm probably going to own half this town or more. Duval Mining will be coming this way soon, as soon as I'm finished in McSchowell County that is. You both will be begging me for a job. Oh, yeah, I don't believe in integration, so your precious little genius of a colored girl won't be going to any school that I have anything to do with. Good day to both of you."

"Mr. Blackwater, he just threatened us. He threatened our jobs and he threatened Harlem's education. What kind of a school would be run by a man like that?" Sara said.

"Miss Mason, we're going to have to call a town meeting. We don't want Mr. Duval to know there even is a meeting. I don't trust the sheriff or half of the town council, but I guess we are going to have to

Mary Wagner

trust the people to make the right decisions in this town. If not, there won't be a school, town or any other part of Kolter left if Mr. Duval and his mining company have their way."

Sara said, "next Saturday is the spring dance at the Town Hall. Do you think that would be a good place to address everybody on what we were just told by Mr. Duval? He would have no reason to show up at the dance. We both heard what he said, Mr. Blackwater, and we can't run from this. It's our duty to warn the people here what he intends to do. I would like to let Mr. O'Brannan know ahead of time if it is ok with you."

"Miss Mason, I mean Sara, just call him Brady. Professionalism is ok in school in front of other parents, teachers or the children, but between you and me and Brady, it's a friendship. And yes, I'd rather Brady knew this, it concerns Harlem. Mr. Duval has never met Harlem and he doesn't like her. I think he would really like her if he did meet her. But he forms this repulsive, ignorant premise that he loathes her because she isn't his color. I'll never understand that."

"I don't understand either, Mr. Blackwater. She is just a little girl. Why would a man in his position, with all his money, hate and fear a little girl he hasn't even met. I better get back to class."

That very afternoon Brady went right to Kolter Telephone Company to have them install a phone in his home. He knew the installation wouldn't be overnight because the poles would have to be put in the ground and the telephone wire would have to be strung from pole to pole up that steep mountain. He was ok living by himself, but now he had Harlem and he wanted to make sure she would be safe in case he wasn't home and she needed help.

Brady also thought since he was in town that he would surprise Harlem and pick her up from school. He was a little early so he thought he would go to Mama Lucille's restaurant, have a cup of her delicious coffee and check up on Coop to make sure he was still doing a good job for Mama Lucille.

Brady walks up and sits down at the counter. "Hi, Miss Lucille. I'll just take a cup of that fine coffee of yours. I'm pickin' Harlem up from school today. I'm a little early. Thought I'd stop in and check up on your new employee while I'm here. How's Coop doin?"

"Mr. Brady, that man is one of the finest employees I have. He's never late, does anything I ask him to do, but most of all – he minds his own business. I thank you for sendin' him my way."

"Miss Lucille, that sure makes me feel good. There he is now. Hey Coop, how you doin'?"

"Hey Brady. Good to see you. Where's Boone? Ain't seen him for a few days."

"We got us a big order from a guy down in Meeks County. He's goin' to build a big general store in town. He heard about us, and Boone's gettin' his order for lumber today."

"Well ain't that some good news Brady. That kind of makes up for my Velma and your Harlem's bad news at school."

"What are you talkin' about Coop? Harlem is happier than she's been in quite a while," Brady said.

"I take it she ain't told you what happened at school the other day," Coop said.

"Yeah, she was a little upset 'cause the school bus had a flat tire. She knew I would be worried about her bein' late. That's one reason I'm in town today. I knew I better have a telephone at home in case somethin' like that happens again."

"Oh, never mind then Brady. You say hi to Boone when you see him."

"Wait a minute Coop. What do you know that I don't know?"

"Look Brady. I don't want to get Harlem in trouble," Coop said.

"Now you got to tell me what you're talkin' about or I'm goin' to camp out here 'til you do," Brady said.

"There's this new gym teacher at school. All the kids seem to be scared of him. You know —one of those tough-talkin' teachers from up North. I don't know the whole story, but he called Velma, Tiny, and he called Harlem, Sambo. Harlem took up for both of them and told him that those weren't their names. He got mad because she spoke up and he gave them both detention. The bus didn't have a flat tire and they got to stay again tonight for punishment. Velma just cries and cries. The kids call her Tiny now instead of fatso. She doesn't even want to go to school anymore," Coop said.

Brady didn't say a word at first. Mama Lucille looked at Coop and shook her head, then she said, "Brady, Brady, now don't do anything you're goin' to be sorry for. Just sit here for a few minutes and cool yourself down."

Brady looked at Coop. "Coop, what's his name?"

Mama Lucille looked at Coop and shook her head again. "Gee, Brady, I can't recollect his name right now," Coop said.

Brady got close to Coop's face. "I'm only goin' to ask you one more time. What is his name?"

"His name is . . . his name is Roy, Roy Finch."

Brady turned around and started walking out the door.

Mama Lucille hollered after him. "Brady, Brady, don't you do anything you're goin' to be sorry for. You hear me. Oh Coop, how I wish Boone was here. He's the only one who can talk some sense to him and calm him down."

chapter 23

BRADY PULLED INTO the school parking lot, slammed his truck door and started walking straight to Mr. Blackwater's office. Sara was in the next room teaching her third grade class when she looked out the window and saw Brady get out of his truck. She thought he looked like a wild bull getting ready to charge. She excused herself from her class for a minute and thought maybe she could head him off from talking to Mr. Blackwater. She was too late.

Mr. Blackwater greeted Brady. "Brady, what brings you here today?"

Brady had this vacant stare at Mr. Blackwater. "Floyd, where is Roy Finch?"

"He's probably in the auditorium. He just finished his last class. Why Brady?"

Brady said nothing and walked out. Just then Sara caught up with him.

"Brady, please don't do anything you're going to be sorry for. Please. Just stop for a minute," Sara said.

"Sara, why didn't you tell me the truth the other night. He embarrassed Harlem and Velma by callin' them names. Why didn't you tell me?"

"Brady, Harlem begged me not to tell you. She said you would be disappointed in her. She was very upset that you would be hurt more than she was," Sara said.

"How could I be disappointed in her, Sara? I have regretted for years not talking to my son. Then it's too late. He comes home in a box. Harlem is all I have left of my son, David. I'll never let anyone hurt her."

Just then Mr. Blackwater catches up with both of them knowing something is wrong. Brady heads for the auditorium while Sara tells

Mr. Blackwater what Mr. Finch said to Harlem and Velma and how he scares the other children.

Brady enters the auditorium and confronts Mr. Finch. "Are you Roy Finch?"

"Yeah, and who wants to know?"

Brady balls up his fist and says. "My right fist wanted to meet you." He punches Mr. Finch and he falls to the floor holding his nose which is bleeding.

Brady looked down at Mr. Finch and said, "you ever call my Granddaughter Harlem, or Velma or any kid at this school a name, I'm goin' to introduce my left fist to you."

Mr. Finch saw Mr. Blackwater and Sara enter the auditorium and he said, "you saw him punch me. Call the sheriff. I want this big dope locked up."

"There you go again Finch – name callin'. My left fist wants to meet you real bad," Brady said.

Mr. Blackwater looks down at Mr. Finch. "I want you out of my school today. You've got a lot to learn about respect. It's earned Mr. Finch. I have no respect for you. I don't know how you taught children up North, but that's not how we teach our children here. Get out of my school. I never want to see your face around here again. Looks like your mouth can't bully a real man, only little children. Now get out. And Miss Mason and I didn't see a thing."

Mr. Finch got up. "I'll go but I'm not leaving town. You haven't seen the last of me. And Brady, you know that old saying – "like father, like son". In your case, it's "like son, like father". By the way, I heard that color rubs off."

Brady grabbed Mr. Finch, threw him up against the wall. Mr. Blackwater and Sara had to beg Brady to take his hands from around his neck. Sara pleaded, "Brady, please. You're going to kill him. He's worthless, you're a good man and Harlem needs you. She's lost everyone but you. Please Brady."

Brady finally let him go. "You get out of this town tonight if you want to be breathin' fresh air tomorrow. You hear me!!"

Mr. Finch finally met more than his match. He was shaking, but he still tried to sound tough. "Yeah, yeah. This worthless hick town won't be around that much longer anyway."

Brady looked at him. "What do you mean by that?"

Mr. Blackwater said. "Let him go Brady. Let him go."

Mr. Finch walked out.

Sara looked at Brady. "Brady, Mr. Blackwater and I need to talk to you about a conversation Mr. Duval had with us the other day. Let's go back to the office."

While in the office, Mr. Blackwater and Sara told Brady that Mr. Duval just about said that there wouldn't be much left in the town of Kolter when he and his mining company got finished with it. Brady did decide with them that the Saturday night spring dance would be the best time to talk to the people of Kolter.

"I think I'll take Harlem out of class a little early tonight. Her and I have a lot to talk about," Brady said.

"Now Brady, she doesn't know you know anything regarding Mr. Finch's punishment that he gave her. She's going to be upset because she knows she is supposed to go to detention tonight," Sara said.

"Sara's right, Brady. Harlem follows rules and you're going to ask her to break one," Mr. Blackwater said.

"I'll worry about that later. I'm going to get her now. She's goin' to have to learn to trust me and tell me about problems that happen in her life now and later."

Brady stood outside Mrs. Hollins fifth grade class waiting for the children to be dismissed. He peeked into the window in the door and noticed how attentive Harlem was in listening to Mrs. Hollins giving instructions on what homework the children had to do. He noticed how much younger Harlem looked compared to the other fifth graders but she seemed more alert and tuned in than the rest of the class. He talked to himself for a few seconds and said. "Kathleen Rose, I wish you were here to see our beautiful little granddaughter. She's so smart, just like you were. They even put her up two grades and maybe one more in September. Please pray for me Kathleen. I'm goin' to need all the help I can get to raise her by myself."

Just then the last bell rang and the children filed one at a time out the door.

Harlem looked up and was surprised to see Brady leaning up against the wall. "Grandpa, how come you're here?"

"I went to the phone company earlier and put in for a new telephone for us. I figured it's about time I got one. You can even call your friends from school now. I'm drivin' you home today. Won't be any reason to worry about another flat tire on the bus," Brady said.

Harlem's eyes started to tear up. Brady's heart sunk. It hurt him to see her fill up with tears. She knew he caught her in a lie. "Grandpa, I lied about the flat tire. I didn't want you to hate me because I did something bad in school. I got detention for two days."

Just then Sara entered the hallway. The children were already out the door. She didn't want to embarrass Brady and Harlem, so she stood back where she couldn't be seen but she still could hear the conversation.

Brady picked Harlem up and kissed her tears. "Harlem, I could never hate you. Right now you're the best thing that has happened in my life. I know what Mr. Finch said to you and Velma and it was wrong. I am proud of you for taking up for yourself and Velma. I just want you to remember that you can tell me anything. I don't care what it is. From the first time I saw you get off that bus, I fell in love with you. You can never hate a person you love that much. When I saw your beautiful blue eyes and that little smirk when you smiled, I saw my David —your daddy when he was a little boy. Is everything ok now, because Blue Boy is out there in the truck waitin' to lick your face too death. Are we ready?"

"Yes sir. Grandpa, my mother used to read me about "Little Black Sambo". He was from the country, India. He wasn't a colored boy from here. I know Mr. Finch was calling me Sambo because of the color of my skin. I just didn't think it was nice to call me that in front of all the other kids. And he called Velma, Tiny. Tiny is this fat boy from the comic books that the other kids made fun of. I didn't mean to cause trouble," Harlem said.

"Well, the problem has been straightened out. The only trouble that was caused was by Mr. Finch. Oh, and there is one little thing I forgot to tell you. Mr. Finch won't be teachin' at Kolter anymore."

"Why Grandpa, what happened?"

"He slipped on the floor in the auditorium and broke his nose. I heard he's gone back North to start some kind of a new business."

"Now I'm really happy Grandpa!"

Sara had to wipe the tears from her eyes. She watched this big, strapping, strong man show such caring and tenderness to this little girl.

chapter 24

WHEN BRADY AND Harlem pulled up to their home, they noticed Boone's truck out front. Boone came running out of the house pretty shaken up and said, "Brady, trouble is comin' to Kolter!"

"Hold on Boone, take a breath. What are you talkin' about? Harlem, you go inside and start your homework."

"Yes sir."

"Remember that lumber we delivered to Mrs. Higgins over on Stoneface Mountain. I don't think we'll be buildin' that room for her now."

"Why, did she change her mind or somethin'?" Brady asked.

"Brady I don't know what's goin' to happen now. That ridge right next to her has two front-end loaders and two huge excavators sittin' on it. There are big crates labeled "dynamite". Guess what name is on those boxes?"

"I bet I know Boone – Duval Minin' Company. He threatened Mr. Blackwater because he couldn't bully him into puttin' his son in the class he wanted him in. He just about told Mr. Blackwater he was goin' to own half the town before summer was over. We were goin' to wait until the spring dance Saturday to talk to the people and let them know what's goin' on, but it looks like we're goin' to have to have a meetin' real quick."

"Brady, what about tomorrow night. It's Wednesday, Bible study at the First Christian Church. A lot of town folk come on Wednesday nights."

"You're a smart man Boone Jackson. You don't think that old church will burst into flames if you and me show up, do you?"

Boone laughed. "I pray directly to the Man above. And I know how Kathleen used to sit and say her prayers on that pretty cross with the string of beads on it. I know those prayers were for you Brady."

"Those beads and cross were called a rosary Boone. You're right. My Kathleen said a lot of prayers for me. I guess this town could use some prayin' now. I'll go into town early tomorrow and talk to Preacher Jacob at church to see if he's ok with us talkin' to the congregation to let them know what is goin' on. First I'll stop and see Mr. Blackwater," Brady said.

"Are you goin' to let Harlem know about this situation? Boone asked.

"She'll find out soon enough at church tomorrow night."

The next day Brady drove Harlem to school and also informed Mr. Blackwater about the meeting that he wanted to have that evening at church concerning the new information about the Duval Mining Company. Brady then went to Preacher Jacob's home and knocked on the door. "Brady, what brings you here? I better look up – a piece of Heaven might be falling my way" Preacher Jacob said. They both laughed.

"Jacob, we both have known each other since we were boys. I know you love Kolter as much as I do. Well, the devil has come a knockin'."

"Brady, what in the world are you talking about?"

"Have you seen the mountains in McSchowell County lately?" Brady asked.

"Oh, Brady, I most certainly have. It's an abomination against nature and God. Whatever company removed that beautiful mountaintop to find coal left that mountain in a hideous state of dirt and rubble."

"Well Jacob, that word you used, abomination. Well its comin' to Kolter. That's why I'm here. I was wonderin' if I could take a few minutes of your Bible study time and talk to your congregation tonight?"

"Are you sure Brady, that's going to happen here in Kolter?" Jacob said.

"You know the principal of Kolter Elementary, Mr. Blackwater and Miss Sara Mason, the third grade teacher."

"I most certainly do. Why?" Jacob asked.

"A man with the last name of Duval is in charge of what is happenin' in McSchowell County. He told Mr. Blackwater and Miss Sara

Mason, that before summer is over he will own half this town. And you know that after he finishes his surface minin' for coal, Kolter County is goin' to look like McShowell County does now. Is that what you want?" Brady asked.

"Now you know better than that Brady. Bible study starts at seven. You and anybody else that wants to talk can come. The more the folks in Kolter know about this, the better. See you tonight," Jacob said.

"Thanks Jacob, I owe you one."

"How about I see that face of yours in church with your new granddaughter one Sunday?"

"Well, you knew Kathleen was Catholic, so is my granddaughter," Brady said.

"Have you had a chance to take your granddaughter to the Catholic Church? Isn't it about fifty miles from here? All I'm saying is you both are welcome to come here. God is everywhere, doesn't matter what religion you are. See you tonight Brady."

Brady came on home and let Harlem ride the bus home that day. It was a good thing he did come home early, because the telephone people just finished putting the poles up and needed to get inside his home to install the phone and wiring.

When Harlem came home, she waited until after supper and the dishes were done to talk to Brady. "Grandpa, do you know what tomorrow is?"

"Let me think. Tomorrow is the day Blue Boy gets a bath?"

"No, Grandpa."

"Tomorrow is the day Boone takes a bath? I shouldn't have said that, he would probably get his feelins' hurt if he heard me say that," Brady said.

"No, Grandpa."

"Harlem, I know what tomorrow is. It's April 1st, and It is your mama's birthday."

"I knew you would remember. I knew it."

"Come on out in the shed for a minute. I got somethin' I want to show you," Brady said.

Brady uncovered the gravestone for Harlem's mother he was working on. The stone matched her father's gravestone, even the exact color. Her name was carved in beautiful letters across the stone,

Belinda Allyson O'Brannan

Born April 1, 1932

"I know I told you that you could help me carve the letters, but with you goin' to school and me and Boone deliverin' all this lumber, I figured I'd surprise you. Hope I did," Brady said.

"Grandpa, the letters and numbers are beautiful. The stone matches my Daddy's stone. You even carved those pretty roses on the stone. Thank you, thank you." She hugs Brady. Just then Boone pulls up in his truck and comes into the shed.

"I didn't want to be late for the meetin' at church tonight. Brady you did a good job. How come you left off the (looks at Harlem) that other date that goes after the born date? You know what I mean."

"Boone, if you notice that date ain't on none of my family since David and Kathleen passed."

"Why is that Brady?"

"That date, the day my Kathleen and my David died are two dates I don't want to think about. I want to think about the time they lived and when they came into my life, and how happy their lives were and how happy my life was because they were a big part of it. If Harlem wants me to put that date on her mama's stone, I will. Do you Harlem?" Brady asked.

"No, Grandpa. That was a terrible day that I don't want to remember."

"Harlem, the ground is a lot softer now up at the cemetery. How's this Sunday sound for you and me to bury your mama next to your daddy?" Brady said.

Harlem said, "I can pick some of those little crocus flowers that just came up. They're purple, white and yellow. I can make some nice bouquets for Mama, Daddy and Grandma Kathleen."

"Boy that sounds nice, Grandma Kathleen. She really would have liked to hear those words, Grandma Kathleen, wouldn't she Boone," Brady said.

"Brady, she sure would have. Just wasn't meant to be. Guess we better head on out. Don't like to be late for anything, you know how I am," Boone said.

Brady said, "let's get goin' then."

chapter 25

THERE WAS A large crowd at the church for Wednesday night Bible study. Kolter wasn't that big of a town. Church was a big part of everyone's life in town. Before going into church, Brady, Boone and Harlem stopped by Mama Lucille's to tell her about the meeting. He felt it only right that the colored families of Kolter knew what was going on also. They were farmers, store owners, and just plain neighbors like everyone else in town that contributed to the growth of the town through hard work and paying their taxes. But in back of the church hidden in the crowd stood two men, one slightly familiar face, Roy Finch, and one unfamiliar face, name unknown. No one noticed either one of them.

Of course there were stares when the colored families came in and stood in the back of the church. But most people were wondering what this was all about. Preacher Jacob walked up to the pulpit and led the congregation in prayer – "The Our Father".

Preacher Jacob then said, "I guess you all are wondering what is going on. There won't be any Bible study tonight. There is a problem that I was told about yesterday that will affect every man, woman and child here in town. You all know Mr. Brady O'Brannan. I'm going to let him explain the situation to all of you. Brady, I think it would be better for you to come up here to address the congregation."

Brady walks up to the pulpit.

"How many of you people out there are familiar with what is going on in McShowell County?" Brady asked.

Quite a few people raised their hands and a few shouted out, "it's a disgrace."

"Yes sir it is a disgrace. Well for those of you who don't know what's going on, I'm goin' to try and explain it to you because it's happening at Stoneface Mountain now which ain't too far from Kolter. There's this minin' company –Duval is the name of it. What they're goin' to do is try and buy your property for next to nothin'. They will buy what property in town that they can so there won't be anybody complainin' about what they're goin' to do to the mountains surrounding Kolter," Brady said.

Boone shouted out, "tell them Brady what our beautiful mountains are goin' to look like! And tell them about the creeks and how they'll be empty of that good tastin' trout. Tell them Brady!"

Brady talked to the people and said, "the Duval Minin' Company comes in and burns all the lumber on the mountain. That rich topsoil we got here that produces our crops for our animals and our huge gardens is removed. The minin' company's next step is to use explosives and blast away the rocky ridges so they can get to the coal on the mountain surface. Now they're not finished yet. All that rock they blast has to go somewhere. They dump this rock in hollers, and valleys and any streams or creeks. There goes any hope of catchin' those trout you all like to eat, because they will eventually die. While they're doin' all this blastin,' animals are dyin.' Our beautiful trees, flowers and forest will be gone. If the people in this town stick together, we can fight these people. They can't make you sell. It takes one person to sell, then another one sells, then another one sells. Don't let the Duval minin' company ruin our beautiful town."

Someone from the crowd shouted. "How do you know for sure they're comin' here?"

Mr. Blackwater stood up. "You all know who I am. I was threatened by Mr. Duval in person. What we talked about was a private school matter that he and I did not agree on. He assured me that before summer ends he will own half of this town and I would be begging him for a job. Is that a good enough answer for you?"

The congregation started talking loudly amongst themselves.

An older man stood up and said, "don't they have to come back and fix the land again?"

Brady answered that question. "Did they fix the land in McShowell County back to what it was –NO! The town of McShowell is like a

ghost town and you all know how beautiful the mountain that surrounded the town was. Look at it now. They got their coal, sold it,
made a lot of money, destroyed people's lives, killed animals, then they
left. Is that what you people want to happen here in Kolter? If that's
not what you people want, then we have to stick together. We have
to look out for each other. As soon as you are confronted by one of
Duval's heavy handed men and asked to sell your property, get in touch
with one of us, any of us. We can stand together as one. We can fight
them. They can't hold your arm and make you sign your property deed
over to them. Before it goes that far, holler for help."

Mr. Blackwater stood up again and said, "let me see the hands of
those in favor of standing up to the Duval Mining Company?"

Everyone in the congregation raised their hand.

Mr. Blackwater asked again, "how many people are against standing together as one and fighting the Duval Mining Company?"

No hands were raised.

Mr. Blackwater had a few more comments to make. "I propose
we have a committee headed by Brady. This committee will be made up
of several men that you will be able to call in case you are approached
by someone from the Duval Mining Company offering to buy your
property. Can I have a show of at least a dozen men to serve on this
committee? This committee won't be just you white folk that are here,
but the committee will be made up of our colored neighbors, who are
affected by this threat as well as our Indian neighbors. So if anyone here
is against this part of the committee proposal, there's no need to raise
your hand – just leave, because I personally don't consider you part of
this community."

No one left the meeting. Finch and the other guy he came to the
meeting with slithered out the door like the snakes they were. More
than a dozen men raised their hands and a committee was formed.
The people in town knew who they could contact in case they were
confronted by anyone. This made the people feel more at ease in case
trouble would arise.

Preacher Jacob got up and thanked Brady and Mr. Blackwater, and
the congregation and all the other people who weren't members for
coming. There was a prayer of thankfulness from the preacher and
everyone left the church.

chapter 26

IT WAS SATURDAY night and Harlem was as excited as her grandpa. The spring dance was being held at the Town Hall; but more importantly, Saturday was closer to Sunday. Sunday is the day her grandpa promised Harlem that they could bury her mother and put up her new stone. The spring dance was being held a little earlier than usual. Most of the farmers picked this date so that they could take advantage of the good planting weather.

The dress Harlem was wearing was from the only dress shop in Kolter – "Lola's". Lola's had all sizes from a little girl on up to women's sizes. The dress was white, with red ribbon woven around the neck, sleeves and around the waist and tied around the back with a red bow. She had a red fake flower on the side of her hair which she wore down. There were no pigtails tonight.

Brady wore what he wore the day he met Harlem at the bus station. He had on the black buckskin jacket with the fringes on it, his denim overalls, light blue dress shirt, and that beautiful bola tie. Of course, Brady never went anywhere without his black leather cowboy hat. He was a very handsome man.

When Harlem walked down the narrow steps from her bedroom, Brady couldn't take his eyes off of her. "Harlem, you look so pretty tonight. You're goin' to be the prettiest girl at the dance."

"Grandpa, you're just trying to be nice. But thanks for saying that. You're going to be the handsomest man at the dance. Miss Sara will be with the most handsome man in Kolter County."

"And you're just sayin' that to be nice. They're a lot of handsome men in Kolter for a pretty woman like Sara to pick from."

"There's none as nice as you. You're the best grandpa in the whole state of West Virginia."

"I hope I can live up to those words. We better be goin'. We have to pick up Miss Sara. Boone is goin' to meet us at the Town Hall. I hope he leaves that old coonskin hat at home. That might scare some of the women away when it's time for dancin'." They both laughed and went out the door and got into the truck. Blue Boy jumped up and looked out the window as Harlem waved good-bye to him.

Brady stopped and picked Sara up for their real first chaperoned date. Brady knocked on the door and Sara opened the door. "Sara, you look beautiful. How lucky can this old mountain cowboy get? I've got the two most beautiful women with me from Kolter County." Brady couldn't keep his eyes off of Sara either. He almost drove into a ditch twice.

Sara's dress was a light blue, almost matching Brady's shirt. Her dress had a big white collar with a white belt to match her small waist. Her hair was down and flowing like strands of sunlight. For the first time in years, Kathleen wasn't on his mind.

Boone was waiting in the parking lot for Brady. Of course, he had on his coonskin hat, but Brady had to admit he did look clean and well-shaven. His clothes were a little wrinkled but they were clean.

When Harlem got out of the truck, Boone said," better watch her tonight Brady, some boy is goin' to snatch her up as pretty as she looks. Better keep an eye on her."

"Oh, Mr. Boone, I'm too young for a boyfriend and I don't want any," Harlem said.

"See how smart she is Boone. You're always tellin' me how smart she is. I don't have to worry about any boy snatchin' her up tonight," Brady said.

Boone looks at Sara, "Miss Sara, may I say you look so pretty tonight. But you're walkin' in with the wrong man. It should be me."

Everybody laughs.

"Thank you Boone for your comment, but I bet you're going to have a hard time keeping the ladies away from you tonight," Sara said.

Harlem said, "Mr. Boone, you even smell good tonight."

Boone replies, "why thank you pretty little girl, can I escort you in tonight?"

Harlem puts her arm out for Boone to hold. "Yes you can Mr. Boone."

The band that night was a group of men and one woman that could sing country songs almost as well as the recording artists themselves. They were called "The Mountain Express".

Brady and Sara mingled with some of the people in town that they knew. Harlem talked with some of her classmates that were there. Boone finally took that coonskin hat off and hung it on a hook where some of the people hung their coats and jackets.

After about a half hour, Brady finally got the nerve to ask Sara to dance. The song was "I Fall to Pieces" by Patsy Cline, but sung by the girl in band.

As they slow danced, which is as close as they had ever been, they just stared into each other's eyes. Then they put their heads together as they danced. Sara finally started talking. "Brady, you're one of the nicest men I have ever met. When I'm with you, I feel safe. I just . . . I just love being in your arms right now."

"Sara, I don't want the song to end, because I won't be able to hold you until the next slow song. Since I first met you, I wanted to be in your life. I hope you don't kick me out of your life any time soon."

Sara looks into Brady's eyes. "That's the least of your worries."

They continue to dance until the song ends. Brady walks over to the punch bowl and notices Harlem standing at the dessert table talking to Velma and her mother. Brady walks over to talk to Velma's mother. Just then the band started playing Marty Robbins song – "A White Sport Coat and A Pink Carnation".

Brady asked Mrs. Little, "where's Coop tonight Mrs. Little?"

"He's still workin' at Miss Lucille's restaurant. He should be gettin' off soon. He said he'd come right over after the restaurant closes. Doesn't that singer sound just like Marty Robbins, Brady?"

"He sure does Mrs. Little. And Velma, you look so pretty tonight."

"Thank you Mr. Brady."

"Brady, I want to thank you for gettin' Coop that job at the restaurant. It changed him and our whole life. I just can't thank you enough."

"No need to thank me. Miss Lucille is the one who gave him a chance."

Right at that moment, someone ran into the Town Hall and hollered "FIRE, FIRE."

Brady told Sara to watch over Harlem and asked Boone to look after them and see to it that they got home safe if he didn't return. Several of the men belonged to the Kolter Volunteer Fire Department and had to stop at the fire station to get the fire truck and pumper truck so they could put the fire out once they found it.

In the meantime, Brady took a few of the men in his truck to find the fire. The fire was at Mama Lucille's restaurant. All Brady could think about were the people who were working there. The only good thing was it was closing time and there were no customers. Flames were coming through the roof, windows, and everywhere. There was a canvas cover over a chair in front of the restaurant. Brady doused with water, put it over him, kicked the door down and ran in. The smoke was so overwhelming he could hardly breathe. Brady found Mama Lucille and dragged her outside. He doused the canvas with water again then went back inside after getting his breath. He knew Coop had to be in there somewhere.

Just then the fire and pumper truck pulled up to the restaurant. At the same time Boone pulled up with a frantic Sara and Harlem in the front with him and Mrs. Little and Velma, also frantic, were in the back pickup part of the truck.

The two men Brady brought with him were tending to Mama Lucille. The ambulance was on its way.

Harlem screamed. "Where's my grandpa? Grandpa, Grandpa!"

Sara held her close and said, "you're grandpa is going to be ok Harlem. He's going to be ok."

"I can't lose Grandpa too, Miss Sara!"

Sara held Harlem's face in her hands. "You're not going to lose him, you're not, believe me you're not."

Mrs. Little and Velma were also screaming for Coop.

Velma screamed, "Daddy, Daddy, please come out of there!"

Her mother tried to comfort her knowing things did not look good.

Just then, Brady comes out with Coop over his shoulder. Brady is overcome with smoke. Coop just lays motionless as Velma and Mrs. Little look on with terror on their faces.

Velma was still uncontrollably crying, "Daddy, Daddy, don't leave us, please we need you!"

Mrs. Little was also crying, "Coop, please, you come so far, me and Velma need you!"

The ambulance drivers pull up and start working on Mama Lucille and Coop.

Brady was black and full of smoke but was coming around. He was given oxygen by the ambulance drivers along with Mama Lucille and Coop.

Harlem and Sara run over to Brady to hug him. He puts his hand up and tries to say no.

Brady finally says, "I'm fine. I don't want you two ruinin' those pretty dresses."

Sara says, "Brady, these dresses can be washed. We're giving you a big hug whether you want it or not!"

"Grandpa, don't do that anymore. I can't lose you too. Promise me."

Brady said, "I promise little one, but if somebody needs my help, I have to help them. I can't turn my back. You know me by now."

Harlem hugs Brady. "I love you Grandpa."

Brady hugs Harlem and holds Sara's hand and looks at both of them. "I love you too Harlem and it's a privilege to be in both your lives and it looks like the Good Lord wants me in your lives a little bit longer."

Boone rushes over to Brady and hits him on the side of his arm with his coonskin hat. "Don't you ever do nothin' like that again without me. You hear me Brady. Never again!"

"Boone how's Miss Lucille and Coop?" Brady asked.

"Miss Lucille is comin' around but Coop is havin' a hard time gettin' that smoke out of his lungs. And there's a bigger problem Brady."

Boone whispers in Brady's ear, "looks like Coop got beat up. Ain't from the fire or smoke. He got beat up real bad Brady. I was talkin' to the sheriff and he said he'll look into it, but you know he don't care about Coop."

"Well, I'll tell you who's goin' to look into it, me. I'll get Mr. Blackwater and a few other people from the committee and, by golly, we will find out what happened. You tell Mrs. Little and Velma I'm goin' to try and get to the bottom of what happened here tonight. Would you take Mrs. Little and Velma home? Tell them I'll take them to the hospital tomorrow. Thanks, Boone."

"Sara I'm sorry how the night turned out. I hope I can make it up to you one day."

"Brady, are you serious? You just saved two lives tonight and I'm going to be mad because I didn't get my second dance with you? Brady, I thought you knew me a little bit better than that," Sara said.

"Sara, I know how caring you are, but I am still going to make it up to you. How about we all go home now. There's a lot that I got to get done tomorrow, right Harlem," Brady said.

"Grandpa, we can wait for what we were going to do tomorrow until you feel better and have all the smoke out of your lungs."

Brady said, "I'll feel a lot better when I see that sun come up tomorrow morning."

Just then one of the ambulance drivers came over to ask Brady if he was ok.

"Don't you boys worry about me. You just take care of Miss Lucille and Coop."

The ambulance driver said, "Mr. O'Brannan, if you wouldn't have carried those two people out, they would have died."

"Son, it wasn't their time to die. Now you get them both to the hospital so they can get cared for."

chapter 27

THE NEXT MORNING around six thirty there was a knock at Brady's door. Brady jumped out of bed, put his clothes on and went over towards the window by the door to see who in the world would be visiting that early in the morning. When he looked out the window, the man's back was toward the door. He had no idea who it was, so he got his rifle ready in case it was trouble.

Just then Harlem, still half asleep, came down the stairs. "Grandpa who is it?"

"I don't know Harlem. You get back upstairs until I tell you to come down. Go on now."

The man knocked again. Brady opened the door slowly with his rifle pointed at the man.

"Mr. I don't know who you are, but you got a lot of nerve knockin' on my door this early in the mornin'."

"Sir, I don't blame you, but please don't shoot. I'm Detective Manny Lopez of the New York City Crime Unit. You must be Mr. Brady O'Brannan, Harlem's grandfather."

Detective Lopez put his hand out to shake Brady's hand.

"I'll be darned. You're that Officer Lopez Harlem talks about all the time. You know you saved her life. If it wasn't for you she would be stuck in some God forsaken home and probably mistreated. But you never stopped until you found her family, which happens to be just me. I am proud to shake your hand. Wait until she sees you."

"I heard from quite a few of the people in town that you saved a couple of lives last night Mr. O'Brannan."

"Mr. Lopez, anybody would have done what I did."

"Please call me Manny, Mr. O'Brannan."

"Manny, and you can call me Brady. That fire last night was suspicious. Coop, one of the people I carried out was also beat up. There is a minin' company, the Duval Minin' Company that wants to buy up most of the property here in Kolter. They want to strip the tops of these beautiful mountains for coal. I figure it would only be a matter of time before they started heavy-handed tactics on the people to force them to sell. I was goin' to see Coop today. I thought maybe he could tell me who beat him up."

"To be truthful with you, I'm here following a lead from a case in New York. Harlem sent a letter to a good friend of hers, Arlene. She talked about a physical education teacher that scared her. Arlene showed the letter to Sister Delores."

"Oh, I have heard all about Sister Delores too. I heard a lot of good things about her. I wish I could get the chance to meet her too."

"Maybe you will one day. Sister Delores let me read the letter and a name popped up – Roy Finch. I wondered if there could be two Roy Finch's. There was a Roy Finch murdered about three years ago in his apartment in New York. There were a few good leads. There was one man we questioned and he was considered a viable candidate as a suspect. He was an acquaintance of Roy Finch and knew quite a lot about Mr. Finch. Mr. Finch had no family, and it would be easy for anyone to steal his identity. Mr. Finch's birth certificate, high school and college degrees and driver's license were missing. Our suspect was last seen about three months ago at a bus terminal in New York heading to Florida. He may have gotten off somewhere along that southern route," Detective Lopez said.

"I'll be darn. Looks like my Harlem helped catch a criminal."

"She sure did. We just have to prove this is the guy I'm looking for."

Brady hollers up to Harlem, "Harlem there is somebody here to see you, come on down."

Harlem comes down the steps, sees Detective Lopez, and jumps from the last three steps into his arms. "I can't believe you're here. I knew I would get to see my friends again. How are all the sisters, especially Sister Delores and Arlene and ..."

"Now Harlem, Detective Lopez just got here. He drove all day yesterday and all night."

"That's ok Brady. I'm so glad to see you Harlem. I can see how happy you are. Just to see your face with that big smile on it is worth traveling all day and all night."

"I'm goin' to make us a nice big breakfast. This is a special day for me and Harlem anyway. We want to start off with some of the eggs that Harlem's chickens laid, bacon, and biscuits. You just sit down Manny and Harlem can tell you what has been goin' on."

"Do I call you Detective Lopez now?"

"I'll tell you what. We're friends Harlem, just call me Manny."

"I'm just not used to that. How about Mr. Manny?"

"Mr. Manny it is."

"I have over two dozen chickens and I sell their eggs. I take care of them all by myself. My special chicken is Gladys. She belongs to Grandpa. She likes to stay in the house but she can't anymore. She stays with the other chickens in the new house Grandpa built. I love my new school. I passed all these tests and guess what."

"What?" Manny asked.

"Instead of the third grade, I am in the fifth. And if I do really good work, they may put me in the sixth grade next year."

"Sister Delores said you were very smart. She's going to be excited to hear about how well you're doing in school," Manny said.

"And please, Mr. Manny, tell her I really love it here with my Grandpa and my new friends."

"I sure will tell her. She'll be happy to hear how happy you are. But there is something I would like you to do for me Harlem, if it is ok with your grandpa. I have a bunch of pictures I want you to look at and let me know if anyone looks familiar. Is that ok, Brady? There were several people we couldn't find when the incident that took place three years ago happened. I just want to see if Harlem has seen any of these people."

"That's fine with me Manny. I'm sure Harlem is all for helping the police in any way she can. Right Harlem," Brady said.

"Yes sir, just tell show me the pictures Mr. Manny."

Here are the first eight pictures. Do any of these people look familiar to you?" Manny asked.

"No, they are kind of creepy looking."

"Here are the next eight. Anybody look familiar?" Manny asked again.

Harlem's eyes got big and she backed away from the table.

Brady asked, "what's wrong Harlem? You look like you've seen a ghost."

"This is a picture of Mr. Finch."

Manny asked, "Harlem, are you sure this is him?"

Brady looked. "She's got good eyesight. I probably would have missed that picture. He has gray hair and a big gray mustache now."

"Yes, Mr. Manny I am positive this is him. I don't like him. He has dark hair here, but that is his face. He scares me," Harlem said.

Brady asked Manny, "Manny what is this guy's real name?"

"His name is Angelo Risutti. He is wanted in three states for fraud, theft, assault and battery, assault with a deadly weapon and armed robbery. He is a very dangerous man. He's a strong- arm, for hire type of guy. He does whatever it takes to get the job done, if you know what I mean."

"You mean he lied about his name? Harlem asked.

"He most certainly did. He's not even a teacher. Does anyone know where he is now? That tip we got that he was at the bus terminal was too late. We can't let him slip by again," Manny said.

Brady said, "Harlem can you go upstairs and get ready for breakfast?"

"Ok, I'll be right back Mr. Manny."

"I'll be here Harlem."

Brady said, "Last week I had a run in with him. He called Harlem and a friend of hers a name. I confronted him. I didn't say much to him. I just introduced him to my right fist and broke his nose. Mr. Blackwater, the principal, fired him. His last words to me was that he wasn't leavin' town, that I ain't seen the last of him and this little hick town won't be around much longer. He also said some other nasty remarks that don't need to be repeated."

"Believe me Brady, this guy is dangerous. He means what he says. I'm sure he is still in town or in these mountains somewhere hiding, and he probably had something to do with that fire last night and the assault on your friend Coop. He probably was hired by this Duval guy to scare you people into selling your property. He's nobody to fool with. You think your friend Coop saw his face?" Manny asked.

"Manny, there's only one way to find out. After breakfast, we can go to Kolter General Hospital and ask Coop."

"If he did burn that restaurant down and beat Coop up, he's going to finish the job knowing he left a witness who can identify him. We'll have to get protection for Coop and Miss Lucille. What's the law like here Brady?" Manny asked.

"I don't put much faith in the law here Manny. We can talk to the sheriff. Maybe you can talk some sense into him."

I won't be talking to the sheriff. I was given strict orders not to even let him or anybody in the sheriff's department know that I am here for Angelo Risutti. Apparently, my unit thinks somebody from the sheriff's department is trying to hide Risutti and they are taking a payoff for helping him. We don't know who it is yet, but once we get Risutti, he might sing a little bit. I'm sure whoever Risutti is tied up with in the sheriff's department, is also working for Duval. Sometime today, I'll have to put in a call to the West Virginia State Police and let them know the problem," Manny said.

Brady said, "I'm proud to say I know you Detective Manny Lopez. You saved Harlem's life and I know you'll solve this case."

"I hope I don't let you down Brady, I'll do the best I can," Manny said.

Just then there was another knock at the door.

"Come on in Boone. There is somebody here I want you to meet. Detective Manny Lopez, this is my good friend and partner Boone Jackson."

"What do you mean good friend, you mean best friend. Glad to meet you Detective Lopez."

"Just call me Manny, Mr. Boone. I heard about you to through Harlem's letters."

"You can call me Boone, Manny. I hope she said somethin' good about me."

"In the couple of letters I got from Harlem, she only had nice things to say about you Boone. Oh and a lady named Sara that teaches school. You have no worries."

Boone pointed to Brady.

"Brady's kind of sweet on Miss Sara."

"Ok Boone. Manny is here about that teacher that I told you about, Mr. Roy Finch. That's not his real name and the law from New York has been looking for him for three years. They think he murdered Mr. Finch and took on his identity. He might be workin' for Duval to try and get people to sell their property to him by makin' threats to them."

"I figured just as much. I know he probably had somethin' to do with that fire and that beatin' Coop took. I'm headin' on to the hospital with Coop's wife and daughter now. I just wanted you to know Brady so you don't go stoppin' for them. Maybe I'll catch up with you all later. Nice meetin' you Manny, Boone said."

"Same here, Boone. I'm sure I'll see you later."

"I'll get this breakfast goin' Manny, so we can go to the hospital too. Harlem you can come on down and set the table when you get a chance."

"Be down in a minute Grandpa."

"Brady, you don't know how happy I am to see the contentment on Harlem's face. She had such sadness in her eyes, now they sparkle and shine, especially when she looks at you."

"Manny, I can't tell you enough about the joy that little girl has brought into my life. There were times for years after I buried my son, and then my wife died, that I didn't want to see the sun come up. Seein' the sun come up meant that I had to spend another day without my family. Now I'm up first sunrise. I can't wait to see that little face every morning. I feel like I really have a purpose and a reason to try and live as long as I can. I know Harlem needs me, but I need her just as much. I can't ever thank you and Sister Delores enough for bringing us together."

"Just wish it could have happened a lot sooner Brady."

"Harlem, come on down now. Breakfast is ready. We got a lot to do today."

chapter 28

AFTER BRADY AND Manny got to the hospital, they took Harlem to the recreation room where Velma was.

"Harlem, I'm glad you're here. There are a lot of games to play in this room. We'll have a lot of fun. Please stay," Velma said.

"Sure, I would like to stay if it's ok with you, Grandpa."

"Most certainly is ok, Harlem. Mr. Manny and me want to talk to Coop. Sure you don't mind stayin' in this room until we're finished? We won't be long."

"I don't mind Grandpa; there is a lot of stuff in here to play with. I'll be ok."

Brady and Manny went up the elevator and found Coop's room.

Coop's wife was sitting beside him and got up to take a break while Brady and Manny were there.

"Mrs. Little, Coop, this is Detective Lopez from New York Crime Unit. Is it ok for him to ask Coop a few questions?"

"Brady, Coop can't talk to well with that broken jaw. But you and Detective Lopez can ask Coop whatever you want to. We want to know why somebody did this terrible thing to Miss Lucille and him. I want them caught and put in jail. I'll be back shortly," Mrs. Little replied.

Manny looked at Mrs. Little and said, "thank you Mrs. Little. We surely do need all the help we can get to solve this."

"Coop, I have some pictures of some very bad men. Just nod if they look familiar to you," Manny asked.

Manny shows the first eight pictures. Coop shakes his head, no

He shows the next eight pictures. Coop stares for a second, and then he shakes his head again, no.

"Did you see the man who did this to you Coop," Manny asked.

Coop shakes his head for yes. Then he put up two fingers.

"Are you telling me there were two men who did this to you?" Manny asked.

Coop shakes his head, yes.

"Did Miss Lucille see them?" Manny asked.

Coop shakes his head, no.

"Is there any way you can describe either one of them?" Manny asked.

Coop shakes his head, yes.

"What color was the hair?" Manny asked.

Coop pointed to his own hair which was grey.

"Was there any hair on the person's face?" Manny asked.

Coop shakes his head yes and goes under his nose with his hand.

"Are you telling me he had a mustache?" Manny asked

Coop shakes his head, yes.

"Is there anything else Coop that stands out?" Manny asked.

Coop shakes his head yes and points to his nose and a box of white gauze patches on the table.

Brady said, "He had a patch on his nose?"

Coop shakes his head, yes.

Brady looked at Detective Lopez and said, "that's Finch, Manny."

"You mean Angelo Risutti, Brady."

"Finch is a lot easier to pronounce around these parts Manny. Can we go and pick him up?"

"It's not that simple Brady. Not that there are a lot of gray haired guys with mustache's and a gauze patch on their nose, but I'd rather have positive identification. If we could pick him up for some other reason, get his fingerprints and compare them to the fingerprints on the murder weapon, the knife that killed the real Mr. Finch, we not only have him for what he did to Mama Lucille's restaurant and Coop; but we have him for the murder of Mr. Finch. I have the original fingerprints taken off of the knife that killed Mr. Finch with me."

"I don't think there is anybody in Kolter that can tell you for sure if those fingerprints would match," Brady said.

"I'll have to go to Charleston, West Virginia, Brady. There is a big crime lab there. They should be able to match the fingerprints that were taken from the weapon used to murder Mr. Finch to Risutti's fingerprints, if we are able to arrest him and take his fingerprints. It would really be something if we could bring him in here and stand him in front of Coop. Coop could identify him and we could hold him in jail in Kolter until I could get the fingerprints matched."

"Manny, he's goin' to be hard to catch now. He's either a couple of states away, hidin' in the mountains, or Duval is hidin' him at his place."

"Brady, he is eventually going to get caught. He's not as smart as he thinks he is. He has no idea some detective from New York is here looking for him. He doesn't know that you know who he is. He will get caught, I promise you," Manny said.

Brady said, "Coop, I'm hopin' you get better. When we get this guy, Manny and me are bringin' him in personally for you to identify. You take care."

"Coop, the sheriff will be getting an order from the state police to put a Deputy outside your door and Miss Lucille's daughter's home. I can't let him know that I'm involved. That is why I'm bringing in the West Virginia State Police to give that order," Manny said.

Brady and Manny pick Harlem up from the recreation room and drive back to Brady's.

"Manny, why don't you stay with us while you're here?" Brady asked.

"Come on Mr. Manny, please stay with us," Harlem said.

"Tell you what I'll do. I have a place to stay in town and it's close to the sheriff's office; but if I'm here any longer than three days, I'll take you up on that offer."

"Sounds like a deal to me. How about you Harlem?" Brady asked.

"I hope three days goes by fast," Harlem said.

They all laugh.

After they got home and Manny drove off, Harlem went up into her room and got her mother's ashes.

Brady went out to the shed and brought out Belinda's gravestone that he made and he and Harlem drove the pick-up truck to the top of the mountain to the family cemetery.

Harlem picked a bunch of beautiful crocus, mountain violets, and any other beautiful flowers that grew in the mountain that time of the year.

Brady had packed some biscuits and jam and some pop to drink. This would be their little celebration for Belinda. After all, her birthday was a few days past.

Harlem thought it would be a good time to show her grandpa what Mr. Abermann gave her and the letter he wrote to her. She took the broach out of the container of her mother's ashes.

"Mr. Abermann gave this to Sister Delores to give to me last Christmas. Isn't it beautiful?"

"Harlem, beautiful isn't the word. You weren't going to bury this were you?"

"Well, the letter said to put it in a special place. This might help me to be a doctor one day. I don't have a special place."

"Mr. Abermann was very smart Harlem. Someday this broach will be worth a lot of money. You will be able to use it for medical school. I might not be able to save enough money to put you through school. You hide this broach upstairs in your bedroom until I find a safe place for it. Keep that letter with the broach."

"Would you like to read the letter Grandpa?"

"Harlem, I have to be truthful with you. I can't read very well. When I look at the letters, they are backwards. Your Grandma Kathleen tried to help me, but I was too impatient and bull headed to learn. Now I'm embarrassed and ashamed that I can't read. But I don't want to lie to you. You're grandpa can't read."

"I can teach you. Don't be ashamed. I am so proud of you. You are so brave Grandpa. You can do anything, build anything, everything. Nobody else in town is as good as you. And I know somebody else that can teach you, Miss Sara. That's what she does or that's what she used to do at Mama Lucille's restaurant two nights a week."

"Harlem, I don't know if I want her to know. I told you, I'm embarrassed."

"Grandpa, don't be silly. Miss Sara is a nice lady. She doesn't make fun of people. She helps people like you do."

"Maybe we can talk about this another time Harlem. You want to put your mama in the grave I dug now? Afterward we'll put her stone up."

Harlem laid the box with her mother's ashes in the grave very gently.

"Can we pray Grandpa?"

"Of course. I'll say a few words then you can. Dear God, please see that this good woman is joined in Heaven with her husband, my son David. I want to thank you Belinda and David for bringin' this sweet child into my life. I wish Kathleen could have met Harlem. You take care Belinda. Go ahead Harlem and say your piece."

"Mama, I miss you so much. I am glad you are with Daddy now. I wish you could meet Grandpa. You would really like him. Grandma Kathleen is up there too. Maybe you will get to meet her. I love you Mama."

Brady covers the box of ashes and puts the stone in the ground. They eat their biscuits and jam then drive back down to the house.

chapter 29

THE NEXT DAY Brady took Harlem to school that morning because he wanted to let Mr. Blackwater know the information about Angelo Risutti, alias Roy Finch. Brady ran into Sara in the hallway before classes started.

"Morning Sara. Looks like it's goin' to be a pretty day outside."

"What brings you here Brady, and how is Coop doing?"

"Not too good Sara. He can't even talk. His jaw is broke. I'm here because I need to talk to Floyd about information I got on Roy Finch. A detective from New York, Manny Lopez, is investigating him. Seems Roy Finch is just an alias and he's wanted in New York for a murder. Plus, we both figure he's involved in that fire at Miss Lucille's restaurant and Coop bein' beat up Saturday night."

"Brady, that's terrible and scary. I want to know more, but I have to get to my class now. Maybe we can talk later."

"Sara, that little ice cream shop just opened up down the corner from here. Miss Lucille's nephew, Gerald, just opened it. At least I know that Harlem won't be asked to leave like that night at Dave and Mary's restaurant. You know all my life I never cared about how the colored folk felt about bein' turned away until the night I was told by Dave, who is supposedly a friend of mine, that they wouldn't serve Harlem. But, if she wasn't part of me, and she was the granddaughter of some other white person, would I still feel the same or even care? There I go ramblin' on. So how about joinin' me and Harlem for some ice cream? Now if you're busy, I understand. Maybe we can ...."

"Brady, Brady, I'd love to join you and Harlem for an ice cream tonight. I'll leave my car here, and then you can drop me off afterwards.

And about caring, even if Harlem was someone else's granddaughter, that's who Brady is, one of the most caring people I have run into in years. See you tonight."

"See you tonight Sara."

Brady couldn't keep his eyes off of Sara until she turned the corner. It took him a second to remember why he came into the school in the first place.

Mr. Blackwater was sitting in his office when Brady came in.

"Floyd, we have to talk."

"Come on in Brady. Shut the door if you don't mind, and have a seat."

"Floyd, you know as well as I do that fire at Miss Lucille's was no accident. You can look at Coop's face and tell that," Brady said.

"I knew that Brady. I heard about that detective from New York, Manny Lopez, was at the hospital with you asking Coop questions. How did it go?"

"He couldn't talk because of his busted jaw, but the yes and no answers we got out of him about who beat him up and burned the restaurant down all point to Finch. And Finch ain't his real name. His real name is Angelo Risutti. Detective Lopez said a teacher named Roy Finch was murdered about three years ago in New York. When it was time to question this Risutti guy, he was nowhere to be found."

"That was really smart of me hiring a murderer. He had all the qualifications for the job of physical education teacher. He had degrees, references; he shined like a star in my eyes. Boy did I get fooled." Mr. Blackwater said.

"Don't go blamin' yourself Floyd. Anybody in this school or for that matter anybody in this town would have believed what he showed them. The thing is Manny and me both think he's workin' for Duval as his strong arm. I think that fire and Coop bein' beat up was to show the town what's goin' to happen if we don't either sell our property to Duval or cooperate with him."

"You're right Brady. If we got this Finch or Risutti, whatever he calls himself, maybe Coop would be able to identify him."

"That's exactly how me and Manny feel. Manny has the finger-prints from the murder weapon that killed that fellow Finch. If we could just get Risutti behind bars after Coop identifies him, Manny can take his fingerprints and compare them to the fingerprints he has with him. There is a big crime lab In Charleston that can match these fingerprints."

"Brady, what bothers me is what is this Risutti and Duval planning for this town next. I'm going to get our committee together and have these men keep watch for anything suspicious going on in Kolter or anybody looking suspicious. We're going to have to keep this to ourselves. We'll have to patrol our own streets. At this point, I don't even trust the sheriff. Was a deputy put on duty to watch Coop's hospital room or Miss Lucille?"

"Deputys were put on duty to watch Coop and Miss Lucille. It was Manny's idea, but he had to go through the West Virginia State Police for them to give the sheriff the order because he doesn't want anyone to know why he is here. Manny doesn't trust anyone in the sheriff's department right now. The sheriff doesn't even know Manny is here investigating Angelo Risutti," Brady said.

"Brady, we're going to have to vote that sheriff out. The first thing he should have done for Coop and Miss Lucille was put a deputy on guard to watch them, he didn't need any order. He is supposed to protect the citizens. That's why he has a badge on. Did you ever think of running for sheriff? You'd make a hell of a sheriff. If you see Boone, tell him to get the men on the committee together. We'll have our meeting right here in my office tonight."

"How does seven-thirty tonight sound? It's still a little dark outside. And nobody except the committee should be at this meeting, and you know all their names and faces. I'm headin' home. I'm supposed to meet Boone at my shed to cut some lumber for a job we have next week." Brady said.

"Seven- thirty it is Brady. Thanks for the information. See you tonight."

Brady went home after talking to Mr. Blackwater to meet Boone and work on his lumber order that he and Boone had to fill. He explained to Boone that Mr. Blackwater wanted him to get the committee together to meet privately in his office at seven- thirty to discuss how to keep the town of Kolter safe from the likes of Risutti and Duval.

After getting a good part of the lumber order together, Brady went back into town to pick Harlem up from school along with Sara. He was treating them to some ice cream at a new shop that just opened.

Brady felt very nervous. But he was a little more at ease because Harlem was with them.

"Would you girls like to sit in a booth or at the counter?" Brady asked.

"Wouldn't a booth be more comfortable? What do you think Harlem? Sara asked.

"A booth is ok," Harlem said.

They all looked at the menu.

"Grandpa, can I have a double dip of vanilla with sprinkles?"

"You know Harlem that sounds delicious. I'll have the same," Sara said.

"I guess we'll make that three," Brady said.

After giving their orders to the waitress, Harlem noticed a little girl come into the shop that she knew from the meeting Brady called together at church.

"Grandpa, do you care if I talk to that girl that just walked in the shop?"

"Does that girl have a name?" Brady asked.

"Oh yeah, her name is Liza. She's Miss Lucille's granddaughter. I sat with her that night in Preacher Jacob's church when you talked to the people about that mining company."

"Sure, go ahead, but as soon as you see the waitress bring our ice cream, you come back over."

"I will," Harlem said.

All Brady could think of is "what am I going to talk about alone with Sara, especially after Saturday night?"

"Sara, I'm sorry Saturday night got ruined for you," Brady said.

"Brady, you had nothing to do with the events that took place. You saved two lives. In my book, you're a hero."

"I'm no hero, Sara. Anybody would have done what I did."

"No, you're wrong. Maybe Boone, Mr. Blackwater, a few others, but not everybody would have done what you did. And Brady, I meant what I said while we were dancing. You're the nicest person I know. And I loved being in your arms. There, I said it."

"I also meant what I said Sara. I really do want to be part of your life. I never thought I would feel this way again. But it's different this time. Having Harlem in my life gave me a reason to get up in the mornin'. She makes me want to go on livin' when I really didn't want to at times. When I look at you, I feel this inner thing inside my chest that makes my heart feel like it wants to burst with, I don't know, some kind of happy, happy. I can't explain it. I was never good with words." Brady laughs a little and then gazes into Sara's eyes. "I never thought I would feel this way again. And, there, I said it."

"Wow Brady, I don't know what to say except I don't want your heart to burst," Sara laughs, "but it seems like we kind of really like each other a lot. I like "happy, happy". What do you think?" Sara said with a smile on her face.

"I think right now I just want to be in your life, if you'll have me – that is until you get tired of me. Just let me know," Brady said.

"Yes, yes, yes, I want you in my life. There it's settled. Looks like our order is on its way," Sara said lovingly.

Brady calls out to Harlem, "Harlem, the ice cream is here."

chapter 30

BRADY DROPPED SARA off at her car before the meeting and took Harlem to Velma's house. Brady and Sara actually made a date for the movies the next Saturday night. At least Brady felt the relationship was moving ahead even though it was moving in little steps.

That evening the committee met at Mr. Blackwater's office in secret. Boone was in charge of deciding what business, school, or road that each man would be watching. There was no telling what Duval and his hired men would be up to next. Detective Manny Lopez was invited and gave the committee a rundown on the latest about Risutti, alias Roy Finch, and that he and Duval were probably working together. He warned the men that Risutti was dangerous, and if they did find, hold him until he got there and he would arrest him right away. Hopefully, there wouldn't be any trouble on the horizon; but until Risutti was found and locked up, anything could happen. Manny also told them not to let anyone from the sheriff's department know that he was in town looking for Risutti.

After the meeting, Brady picked Harlem up from Velma's house. On the way home, Brady thought he would find out how Harlem felt about Sara.

"Harlem, do you like Miss Sara?"

"Grandpa, she is a nice lady. I sure do like her. Do you?"

"Yes I do Harlem. Can I ask you a question?" Brady asked.

"Of course, Grandpa, you're my Grandpa. Ask me anything."

"Harlem, do you care if I court Miss Sara?"

"What's court mean Grandpa?"

"You never heard that word?" Brady asked.

"No sir, I don't know what that is."

"Maybe they call it somethin' different in New York," Brady said.

"It's when a man takes a woman to a dance or the movies, somethin' like that," Brady said stumbling over his words.

"Oh like Mama told me about how Daddy kept coming into her store in Harlem when he was on leave. She said he finally asked her for a date. They went out and fell in love and got married."

"You got it, a date. Courtin' is a date Harlem. But I'm not marrin' anybody," Brady said trying to clarify what courting was.

"I get it Grandpa. You want to take Miss Sara on a date. I like her. Maybe you can marry her and I'll have a grandpa and grandma."

"Harlem, it's just a date to the movies Saturday night. I'm goin' to ask Boone to come over and stay with you if that is ok with you."

"I like Mr. Boone, he's so funny, but what about Mr. Manny? His three days will be up. He said he would stay with us if he was in town three more days."

"I think he wants to stay in town a little longer than what he expected to stay. Maybe when he finishes his business here, he can stay with us a few days," Brady said.

"Oh boy, we're home. Look Grandpa. Blue Boy is in the window waiting for us."

"He just thinks we got somethin' for him to eat. I've got some soup Boone made the other day. It's not too bad. You can't go to bed on a stomach full of ice cream. I'll heat it up and you eat some of it, ok? I'll feed Blue Boy and you go a start your homework."

"Ok Grandpa."

Brady felt a huge sigh of relief knowing that Harlem does like Sara and doesn't mind that her grandpa goes "courting", or rather on a "date". The one thing he didn't want to do was upset Harlem in any way. He knew she had been through so much in her short life.

The rest of the week seemed like it flew by. There were no incidents in or on the outskirts of the town. Things kind of quieted down. Maybe Rissuti and Duval weren't going to cause any more trouble. The committee rotated every evening and patrolled their assigned areas. There were no problems.

Manny knew better. It was Saturday night and he ran into Brady and Sara taking a walk before going into the movies.

"Brady, good to see you again," Manny said.

"Manny, this is Sara. Sara this is the detective from New York that I was telling you about, Detective Lopez."

"Nice to meet you Detective Lopez," Sara said.

"Nice to meet you too Sara, but please call me Manny."

"I've heard so much about you Manny. If it wasn't for you, Harlem wouldn't be in our lives today."

"I can't take all the credit. She had quite a few people routing for her to find her family. I was just one."

"All the same, I want to thank you," Sara said gratefully.

"Manny, don't you think it's kind of quiet. Is that a good sign or is the train goin' to wreck soon?" Brady asked.

"Brady, I would love to hope it's a good sign, but these kinds of people are ruthless. They lay low then they climb out of their holes and do their dirty business. In your words I think there is going to be a "train wreck". I just don't know where or when," Manny said.

Just then there was a loud noise. The noise came from the direction of the mountains.

Manny turned toward Brady and said, "what in the world was that?"

Brady turned to the direction of his home. He just felt something terrible happened.

"Sara, I hate to do this again, but that noise was an explosion and it came from the mountains. I've got to go and check it out. Boone and Harlem are home."

"Brady, go. Do you want me to go with you?"

"No Sara, Can you get somebody to come and pick you up? And will you call Mr. Blackwater. He needs to get as many of the committee members together as he can and meet me at my house. Thanks Sara."

"Sure, sure, you just go Brady."

"Hold on Brady, I'm coming with you," Manny said.

Manny jumped on the other side of Brady's truck. Brady drove as fast as he could.

Brady looked at Manny and said, "Manny, I didn't want to say anything in front of Sara, but that "train wreck" we talked about earlier – I think it just happened."

"I know it did my friend, I know it did," Manny said.

chapter 3 1

HARLEM AND BOONE were playing a game of checkers when this huge explosion occurred. The explosion shook the house. Some pots and pans fell out of the cupboards.

Boone hollered. "What in the tarnation was that? Are you ok Harlem?"

"Yes, Mr. Boone, but what about Gladys and the other chickens, I hope nothing happened to them!" Harlem said with uneasiness in her voice.

"Harlem, I want you to stay here. I got to go down the mountain a little ways and see what happened. Are you goin' to be ok? And I mean what I say, don't go out that door. I'm sure the folks in town heard that explosion and Brady will be drivin' up that mountain any minute."

"I'll be ok. Don't worry about me. You go see what happened," Harlem said.

Boone grabbed his rifle and went out the door.

Harlem peeked out the window as Boone headed down the mountain. Just then she saw Gladys go off into the woods. The noise really scared Gladys. The other hens were ok. They were locked in the chicken house for the night. Gladys got the run of the yard most of the time since she was like one of the family. Harlem didn't want to lock her up with the rest of the hens.

Harlem opened the door and hollered for Gladys. "Gladys, Gladys, come back here! Gladys, please come back! Blue Boy, I've got to find Gladys. You come with me."

Harlem ran toward the woods where she saw Gladys run to. Blue Boy was right behind her. "Gladys, Gladys, come back girl. If you don't,

I'm going to have to lock you up with the rest of the chickens. Please Gladys!" Harlem begged as she and Blue Boy chased after Gladys.

Gladys then ran into a clearing in the woods. Harlem looked towards the open field and saw two men. One man had a gun pointed at Gladys. The other man stood and pointed his hand toward Harlem. Harlem ran as fast as she could with Blue Boy behind her towards Gladys yelling, "don't shoot, don't shoot!"

The man with the rifle was Risutti. The other man was Duval.

Duval looked at Risutti and said, "you do know who that kid is don't you?"

"I sure do. That's that little colored girl with the smart mouth," Risutti said.

"Wasn't it Brady, her grandfather, that broke your nose?" Duval said cunningly.

Risutti touched the patch on his nose and said, "he sure did break my nose."

"What do you intend to do about it Angelo, she's looking right at us. These hicks in these hills are going to know who put the dynamite here and lit it. She's a witness. She's just a little colored girl Angelo. You know what you have to do." Duval walked away.

Risutti cocks his rifle and shoots. He hits Harlem and she falls to the ground. Risutti hit her in the leg and the blood started oozing out of her leg. Miraculously, Blue Boy layed his body across her leg above the wound. His weight was like a tourniquet and stopped the bleeding only for a while. Harlem was unconscious from losing so much blood. Blue Boy kept barking and would not stop. It was as if Blue Boy was calling for help.

When Boone heard the shot, he frantically ran towards the woods. He could hear Blue Boy's bark and knew which way to run. He looked toward the open field and saw Harlem on the ground and Blue Boy on top of her leg.

"Oh lordy, oh no, please God let her be ok," Boone said with his voice quivering.

Just then Brady and Manny had already gotten to his home and were running towards the open field.

Boone had already put a cloth tourniquet above the bullet hole. He looked up at Brady's face.

"Brady, I'm sorry. She was upset about the chickens and must have run off after Gladys. I told her DO NOT leave the house."

Brady picked Harlem's limp body up and said to Boone, "Boone, I'm not blamin' anybody. I've got to get her to the hospital fast. Hold on Harlem. Ain't nothin' goin' to happen to you. You're goin' to make it girl."

Boone looked at Manny and said, "Harlem must have seen somethin' Manny. Whoever she saw knew she got a good look at them and they shot her."

Manny said, "Boone, we all know who did this and they're going down tonight."

"I'm takin' them down Manny. As soon as I get her to the emergency room, I'm goin' after them. Whoever did this, don't know it, but they saw the sun shine for the last time this mornin'," Brady said in a vengeful voice.

"Being the lawman I am supposed to be, I should be trying to talk you out of it. But you know what Brady? I really don't feel like carrying any extra baggage back to New York. So I hope you clean the trash up. I'll even help you dispose of it," Manny said.

Boone drove all three of them and Harlem to Kolter General Hospital emergency room. The doctors were ready for her. Boone called Sara from Brady's new telephone so she could alert the hospital and let them know Harlem was on her way in. She was taken right up to the operating room.

Sara ran up to Brady. "Brady I'm so sorry. I wish I would have told you I didn't want to go to the movies tonight. What can I do?"

"Sara, don't even think that way. If I would have been home and the explosion went off, Harlem still would have run after Gladys. She's stubborn like me. What happened to her was no accident. Whoever shot her aimed for her. Blue Boy saved her life by lyin' across her legs and stoppin' the bleedin' until Boone got there. What you can do, you're doin' now. You're here. That's what me and Harlem both need, you here," Brady said while wiping the tears from Sara's face.

Just then the sheriff came through the emergency door and said in an unconcerning voice, "I heard there was a shooting and a little girl was shot. Is that right?"

Brady charged at the sheriff because he knew the sheriff didn't care and didn't do his job of protecting the people of Kolter. Manny stopped him and said, "Brady, let me handle this part, and you can take care of the other thing we talked about earlier."

Brady said, "he's worthless Manny. Always was and always will be."

Manny confronted the sheriff. "I didn't catch your name, sheriff. I'm Detective Manny Lopez from the New York City Crime Unit. I was sent here to follow up on a lead about a suspected murderer, Angelo Risutti, alias Roy Finch. Do you know anything about him? There is a cold case still pending in New York for the murder of Roy Finch. I was sent here to find Risutti and bring him back to New York for questioning. And I also think he had something to do with the shooting of Harlem O'Brannan tonight, the fire at Mama Lucille's restaurant and the physical assault on Coop Little."

The sheriff said very nonchalantly, "my name is Sheriff Alan Crump. And if you were sent here to investigate this Angelo Risutti, why wasn't I informed? And this is my jurisdiction not the city of New York. I'll investigate this shooting tonight and the fire. It is none of your business what goes on in Kolter, Mr. big shot detective from New York."

Brady runs over and grabs the sheriff by his shirt collar and in anger said, "you listen here you piece of cow manure for a sheriff. That's my granddaughter bein' operated on now. I already know you ain't goin' to do nothin' about it. You didn't do anything about the fire or Coop. This detective has my say-so and the town's approval to investigate what happened tonight and what happened last Saturday night. Maybe you're the one who belongs behind bars for not doin' your job."

The sheriff hollers out to his deputy, "I want this man arrested for assaulting me. Deputy Rogers, Deputy Rogers. Where the hell are you?"

Manny grabbed Brady off of the sheriff and said, "your deputy went to the bathroom sheriff, and I don't think there is one witness here who saw anything. As a matter of fact, I saw you grab Brady."

Sheriff Crump said, "Detective Lopez, I'll have your badge by the end of the week, and Brady will be locked up before this night is over."

Manny laughed at the sheriff then said, "the end of the week, it's going to take you that long to take my badge? You know, I was informed not to let the law here know why I came, because my unit got information that somebody in the sheriff's office here in Kolter was taking a payoff from Risutti to keep him hidden. And it also looks like that person was probably involved in taking bribes from a certain businessman named Mr. Maurice Duval to scare the people of Kolter into selling their property. That person taking bribes wouldn't be you, would it sheriff?"

"I will have your badge Detective Lopez today as soon as I get back to my office and call the headquarters at Charleston and get a marshall here to escort you back to New York, without your badge," Sheriff Crump said.

Just then Mr. Blackwater and half the committee walked into the emergency room.

Mr. Blackwater had his Indian headdress on and had war paint on his face.

The sheriff looked at him and laughed, "what is this Blackwater, Halloween? You're a sorry sight for a principal of a school."

Mr. Blackwater said, "you're not taking anybody's badge sheriff. If any badge gets taken away, it will be yours. Oh, and this headdress and paint on my face is applied when we Indians are at war. Apparently you don't remember "The Trail of Tears" where my Indian brothers and sisters suffered greatly because of heartless, uncaring men like you. Kolter is at war sheriff. We are trying to save our town and its beautiful surroundings. You know there are people in this town that care for each other and about each other. Most of the people here love Kolter and are good law abiding citizens. We just caught two of your friends, sheriff. They were trying their best to run from that explosion they caused. We know one of them shot Harlem, burned Mama Lucille's place and beat Coop up. They gave you up sheriff and sang like birds. How much did they pay you sheriff to lay low while they tried to scare the folks here into selling their property?"

Manny had to hold Brady back from attacking the sheriff.

Brady leaped towards the sheriff and said, "you low life no account excuse for a human being much less a sheriff. I'm goin' to …"

Mr. Blackwater smiled at Brady and said, "this low life is not worth it Brady. There are two people across the street towards the woods that I think you would be interested in seeing. The committee did well Brady, we got Risutti and Duval."

Mr. Blackwater looked at Manny and said, "Manny you're going to have to arrest the sheriff. I'm afraid you're going to be in Kolter for a while until we vote in a new sheriff. Boone is over there now with his Colt 45 and his rifle, Boone Jr., just waiting for Risutti and Duval to make a move."

Manny walked over and handcuffed the sheriff and read him his rights. Manny turned to Brady and said, "Brady, it's time to take the trash out across the street."

Brady said, "Manny, I have a little girl to raise. If I go across the street, I'll be put away for the rest of my life because of what I'm goin' to do. I can't let Harlem go through that fear that she went through when her mother died. I won't let her go through that again. It's best I don't see their faces. I have a chance with Harlem and maybe somebody else I care a lot about," looking at Sara, "that is if she'll let me into her life. Will you and the boys take them in and lock them up?"

Manny said, "you made the right decision Brady. I'll lock the three of them up. I'll call Charleston tomorrow morning and explain everything. They may send an acting sheriff here until one is voted in. I'll bring Risutti and Duval here tomorrow for Coop to identify and hopefully Harlem will be well enough to identify them also. If everything goes well, I'll be able to take Risutti's fingerprints to Charleston and have them compared to the ones from the murder weapon that killed Roy Finch. That should close that cold case on Mr. Finch."

chapter 32

HARLEM'S OPERATION TOOK quite a while. Doctor Caper, who operated on Harlem, came out into the waiting room to speak to Brady about Harlem's condition.

Dr. Caper, looking very tired said, "Mr. O'Brannan, Harlem is in serious condition. The bullet severed her main artery in her leg and shattered bone in her left thigh bone. It will be a long recovery, but at her young age by this time next year, she will be running and playing normally. She will need therapy for her leg, but other than that she will be her old self again. We had to give her four pints of blood. And whoever put a tourniquet around that leg saved her life."

Brady said, "there were two good friends of mine involved in saving her life doctor. Believe it or not, my dog Blue Boy laid across her leg and the weight of him stopped the bleeding. Then my good, no not good —best friend Boone tied a cloth tourniquet around her leg." Brady shook the doctor's hand and said, "thank you so much Doc, she means the world to me. I don't know what I would have done if she wouldn't have made it."

Dr. Caper looked at Brady and said, "Brady, for three agonizing minutes, I thought she was gone. Her heart stopped beating. All I could think of was how I'm going to tell her grandfather she is gone. We pumped her chest and that little heart started to beat again, then she was back with us."

Brady said again, "thank you so much Doc."

Manny motioned to the doctor to come his way after talking to Brady.

Manny said, "Doctor Caper, I'm Detective Manny Lopez with the New York Police Department, and we think we have the man in custody that shot Harlem. Would it be possible tomorrow afternoon to ask Harlem if she could identify this man and let me know if this is the man who shot her? There is also another man involved that we may bring in also that was with him. Would that be ok?"

Dr. Caper replied, "I think by tomorrow afternoon, Harlem will have a clear mind and be able to identify anybody you bring before her, that is if it is ok with her grandfather."

Brady spoke up and said, "that's really ok with me, and Manny knows that."

Everyone went home but Brady. He wasn't about to leave Harlem alone. He slept in a chair that the nurses brought into the room for him that night.

That morning Harlem opened her eyes and she asked Brady, "Is Gladys ok, Grandpa?"

Brady smiled this big smile of relief and said, "you don't know how happy I am to hear those words. She's fine. Boone is stayin' at the house. She's goin' to stay in the pen with the rest of the chickens, at least for a while. How's my angel feelin'?"

Harlem said in a weak voice, "I feel sore. Some man shot me Grandpa. He looked like Mr. Finch. Why would Mr. Finch shoot me?"

Brady looked at her and said, "I really don't want you to talk Harlem. You need all the rest you can get. Mr. Manny arrested Mr. Finch and another man last night. He is going to bring them both here this afternoon for you to identify. Do you feel up to it?"

"Yes, Grandpa, as long as you are here."

"Oh, I'll be here alright. Don't you worry none about that. Now you rest."

Boone came in about an hour later and whispered, "how's our girl doin' Brady?"

Brady looked at Boone and said, "you old goat. I'm goin' to be grateful to you and Blue Boy for the rest of my life."

Boone said, "what in the world are you ramblin' on about?"

Brady said, "Dr. Caper said Harlem would have bled too death and died if it weren't for the person who put that tourniquet on her leg. That's what I'm ramblin' about. I can't thank you enough Boone. And

I'll just have to buy one of those steaks every once in a while at Tyler's Grocery Market to thank Blue Boy."

Boone laughed and said, "don't buy one, buy two. I like a good steak every once in a while."

Just then Harlem woke up again. She saw Boone and said, "Mr. Boone, is Gladys ok?"

Boone replied, "she sure is. I have to punish her though for runnin' off. She's goin' to have to be penned up with the rest of the chickens for a while. I know you don't like that, but it's for the best so she don't run off again and maybe get hurt."

Harlem replied sleepily, "if you think that is best, then so do I. Grandpa, I forgot to tell you something."

"What did you forget to tell me, Harlem?"

"What I forgot to tell you Grandpa was that Grandma Kathleen wanted me to give you a kiss from her."

Brady thought the anesthesia was giving her hallucinations and said, "Harlem, Grandma Kathleen has been gone for years."

Harlem said, "I know Grandpa. I saw her in Heaven. She was there when I went up on a cloud. She hugged me and said I was pretty and she was so glad to see me. Oh, Grandpa, she had on this beautiful pink dress with a cameo broach that you gave her from your grandmother from Ireland. Her hair had a pink ribbon around it. She was beautiful. It is so beautiful there. She told me to tell you it is ok for you to do what you want to do, and she wants you to be happy again. She told me to tell you not to hold anger in your heart for anyone, and that she did not suffer. In her hands was a beautiful light blue rosary. There is another rosary just like it and she wants me to have it. She said it was in her special hiding place, and that is where I should put my gift from Mr. Abermann. She even knew about Mr. Abermann, Grandpa!"

Brady and Boone both remembered when Kathleen was in the funeral home how beautiful she looked in that pink dress, with the pink ribbon around her hair. Brady also remembered pinning that cameo broach on Kathleen's dress, and putting that blue rosary in her hands.

Brady was speechless and for the first time since her death, he cried. Boone even had to wipe tears away from his face. Brady said, "Harlem, you did see her. She did get to meet you. I wish I could have seen the look on her face when she looked into those beautiful blue eyes. All these years I could never feel any peace about her death. I would feel sick thinkin' that she suffered so at the end. I would feel this terrible guilt because I was still strong and healthy and she was so weak and sick. You just described the beautiful and happy Kathleen that I fell in love with, Harlem. I'm so thankful you got to meet her."

Harlem wasn't finished. She said, "Grandpa, I saw Daddy. He had this army uniform on with a big purple ribbon on his suit. He smiled and said, "I love you. Take care of Grandpa. Tell him I never stopped loving him. My mother was there too Grandpa. I cried and she told me not to cry because she was so happy being with Daddy again. She said I had my Grandpa Brady now to take care of me. She said she will always be watching me from Heaven and she was so happy. She said she missed me, but someday, a long time from now, I'll get to see her and Daddy again. I wanted to stay, but she told me I had to go back because I was needed here. Then the big cloud brought me back here."

Boone looked at Brady and said, "Brady you ok. See David never stopped carin' about you. He always loved you Brady. I told you that over and over again."

Brady looked at Boone and said, "Boone, if Harlem never would have come into my life, I'd still be that grumpy, hateful, old man that would curse God every once in a while for takin' my wife and my boy. Brady do you think God will ever forgive me for hatin' him when they both died?"

Boone looked at Brady and said, "Brady, that man up there don't hate anybody. Get that out of your head. Now we got to be quiet and let Harlem sleep, because Manny's goin' to be bringin' those two scallywags here for her and Coop to identify."

That afternoon Manny didn't bring Risutti or Duval to the hospital. He thought it may be too much for Harlem to deal with just having an operation. He did the next best thing. He got some really good close-up pictures taken by the town photographer.

Mr. Blackwater came to the hospital with Manny, not only to see Harlem and Coop, but also to be a witness along with Brady and Boone that these two men were identified and responsible for what happened to Harlem and Coop.

Harlem did identify the picture of Risutti as the man that shot her. She also confirmed that Duval was the man that was with him that day in the woods.

Coop, still not able to talk, identified the picture of Risutti as the man that beat him up and started the fire. He also confirmed the picture of Duval as the other man that was with him.

Manny and Mr. Blackwater stopped by Harlem's room on the way out and asked Brady to step out into the hall to talk.

Manny said, "we got them both Brady. I'm going to Charleston to find out whether or not the fingerprints from the murder of Roy Finch match the fingerprints I took of Risutti last night. I'm pretty sure they will match, but even if they don't, he's going to be in prison for a long time for his crimes here in Kolter. And Duval is going away for a long time too since he was his accomplice. Duval won't be destroying any more mountains or scaring families into selling their property for quite a while. The sheriff will be keeping them company in prison for the part he played on all of this."

Brady shook his hand and said, "you're a good man, Manny. Thank you and you too, Floyd, for having faith in the people here and fightin' to keep this little town safe from those kind of men."

Mr. Blackwater said, "you just take care of Harlem. I'll ask Sara if she could come over at least twice a week to keep Harlem up on her studies. That is, if it is ok with you Brady. But I have a feeling you'll be quite happy with that situation."

Brady looks down, his face turns red, and he kind of has this little smirk on his face.

Mr. Blackwater looks at Manny and says, "Manny would you ever consider being our sheriff? I asked Brady before and I don't think he is interested."

"Floyd, I'm a New York guy. It's beautiful here and a really nice place to settle down, but right now I'm happy in my job and where I live. Maybe someday I'll be back here. You never know what fate brings. What about you. You helped capture Risutti and Duval. You have the skill and a hell of a lot of knowledge about the law. You should think about it," Manny replied.

"Do you really think the people of Kolter would vote for an Indian to be their sheriff? Even though I'm a Harvard graduate, in their mind

I'm still an Indian. Yes, I did think about it. I even think I would like it, but no, I don't have a chance," Mr. Blackwater said.

Brady said, "If these people don't know by now how much this town means to you, then they're a sorry bunch of neighbors. You have stood up to Duval's minin' company and preserved this beautiful town and the surrounding mountainside. When election time comes around, I'm goin' to make sure your name is on the ballot."

"I'll even come back here and put in a few good words for you, Floyd," Manny said.

"Mr. Blackwater said, "you know, I'm going to give that a lot of consideration."

chapter 33

MANNY NEVER DID get to stay at Brady's house like he wanted to. It seems the folks at the Charleston Crime Unit were able to match Risutti's fingerprints right away. Manny had to take him back to New York to face charges for the murder of Roy Finch. After that trial, Risutti would have to be brought back to Kolter to face charges for arson, attempted murder of Harlem, and assault and battery of Coop. The murder of Roy Finch would probably keep him locked up for the rest of his life if he didn't get the death penalty.

As for Maurice Duval, he was taken to West Virginia State Penitentiary until his trial was held. He was held without bail for being an accomplice and aiding and abetting Angelo Risutti in the shooting of Harlem, the arson at Mama Lucille's restaurant, and the assault and battery of Coop. Mr. Duval won't be blowing up any mountains any time soon. Sheriff Crump is also serving time in the West Virginia State Penitentiary for bribery and accepting payoffs.

Two weeks passed. Harlem finally came home from the hospital. She could barely walk with crutches. The doctor wanted her to stay off those crutches as long as possible and keep her leg elevated as often as possible. Of course, that kept her from going to school. A lot of things changed. Brady gave his bedroom downstairs to Harlem because she couldn't go up and down steps. He slept in Harlem's bedroom upstairs.

Sara was assigned to home school Harlem. She had two free afternoons a week. Of course, Brady was glad to see Sara. On both those days he would cook supper and the three of them would eat together. Since the days were getting quite a bit longer and daylight lasted a few more hours, Brady and Sara would often take walks while

Harlem did her school work. A lot of those days were spent taking Harlem with them and pushing her around the mountain in her wheel chair. Brady and Sara really got a chance to get to know one another.

Harlem enjoyed her time with her Grandpa and Sara. They were like the family she never had. They laughed and talked and enjoyed each other whenever they got together. Harlem would say to herself, "is this what it's like to have a mother and father? I really love being part of a family. I wish Grandpa and Miss Sara would get married."

Harlem was getting a little nervous because she saw the first week of May go by and she still wasn't back to school. But she was really doing great with her crutches.

A birthday celebration was held for Harlem. It was celebrated a little late, but this was the only chance everyone could get together. Harlem turned nine years old on May 1st. To help celebrate her birthday, Sara baked a cake, Boone brought refreshments, and Brady got some special ice cream from Miss Lucille's nephew, Gerald, who opened up that new ice cream pallor where Brady, Sara, and Harlem frequented before Harlem was shot. Even Blue Boy got to eat ice cream and cake. Usually, Harlem celebrated her birthday only with her mother. So she really enjoyed all of this new attention.

Harlem got several gifts, but the most precious gifts were from Grandpa Brady. He gave her that special rosary that Grandma Kathleen told Harlem that she wanted her to have. Brady also hand carved a picture frame from a piece of wood from an oak tree that David used to climb. The frame was for Harlem's precious picture of her and her parents. Of course nobody but Boone and Brady understood or knew about Harlem's little trip to Heaven. He would explain it to Sara much later.

The next morning Harlem asked Grandpa, "when can I start going back to school? May Day is coming up soon and I wanted to be part of it. Instead of that square dancing like Mr. Finch wanted us to do, Mr. Cornish showed us how to dance around the maypole. We practiced going around the maypole and weaving these long streamers in and out. The streamers are all kinds of pretty bright colors like the flowers here on top of the mountain. Mr. Cornish calls this the Maypole dance."

Brady said, "we go to the hospital tomorrow. If they think your leg has healed up, they will take the cast off. But how in the world are you goin' to dance? The doctor isn't goin' to let you run or jump much less dance."

"But Grandpa, the May Day isn't for a few more weeks. You really don't dance, you kind of walk fast and weave your streamers in and out with the other kids. You can come and see it."

"Oh, I'll be there with bells on. I've never seen anything like that before," Brady said.

"Grandpa, why would you wear bells?"

"Harlem, you got to get used to my sayin's. It's kind of like a joke."

"Oh, I get it. Like about throwing that brick at Boone's head. Just a saying."

"You got it now Harlem."

"Grandpa, tomorrow afternoon do you care if Velma comes over with Miss Sara? We are voting for king and queen of the May Day and she has the names on a piece of paper. I want to vote too. I'm sure Sharon Applegate is going to be queen. She is really pretty."

"Well, I think you're prettier than any of those girls at school Harlem."

"That's because you're my grandpa. She is real tall, with long blonde hair. She would make a pretty queen."

"I bet she's not as smart as you are. I bet she ain't as pretty as you are either, is she?"

"No, Grandpa, she is not really smart at all. This contest is about being pretty. And, Sharon is a lot prettier than I am."

"Well, I wish I could vote. Nice, kind and smart like you is the person I would vote for," Brady said.

"Grandpa, do you think you and Miss Sara will ever get married?"

"My goodness girl, you go from one subject to another subject. Why would you ask that?"

"Because you two look like you belong married, that's all."

"Well, Harlem, if I was to marry again, it would probably be Miss Sara. But I ain't gettin' married again. So now, you got nothin' to worry about. Now you go do your homework, then get in bed. We got to get up early and get to the hospital for your appointment. Boone is goin' with us tomorrow," Brady said.

"Goody, goody. I love Mr. Boone, he's so funny," Harlem said.

The next morning Boone showed up to go to the hospital with Brady and Harlem. They had a load of lumber to drop off to a customer pretty close to the hospital and Brady needed Boone to help him unload the lumber.

The doctor removed Harlem's cast, gave her instructions, and told her to be careful with her leg. She still had to stay home from school for a few more days and no gym at school for the rest of the year. Harlem did get approval to walk around the maypole, but no running. This made her really happy because May Day was the last week of May and she would be able to participate in the program.

That afternoon Sara came as usual to instruct Harlem on her subjects from school. She brought Velma with her. Harlem was so glad to see Velma.

"Do you have the voting paper with you Velma for king and queen for May Day?" Harlem asked.

Velma replied, "yes I do. Here it is."

Harlem look at the list of names to vote for queen and her name was on it.

"Who put my name on this list? I don't want it on there. I'm not pretty enough to be queen of the May Day. Now I'm embarrassed," Harlem said.

Velma said, "I nominated you. You are just as pretty as Sharon Applegate. And you are a lot smarter and nicer."

"But Velma, you know I'm not going to win. The other kids are just going to make fun of me."

"Sometimes you make me so mad Harlem. Nobody is going to make fun of you. They make fun of me. You know that. Now if my name was on there, the other kids would laugh," Velma said.

"I'm sorry Velma. Thank you for thinking that much of me. You are a good friend Velma and when I come back to school, the other kids better never make fun of you, I won't let them," Harlem said.

"That's going to be kind of hard to do Harlem, but thanks anyway. Now you better check the box off next to your name," Velma said.

"Harlem laughed and said, "Well, at least I'll have two votes."

While the girls were talking, Brady and Sara went out on the porch for a few minutes.

"Sara, there's somethin' I want you to know," Brady said.

"What is it Brady?"

"I can't read too good, and I was wonderin' if you wouldn't mind helpin' me learn to read better?" Brady said.

"Brady, I have no problem with that. Whenever you're ready, just let me know."

"I wanted to ask somebody from school to help me a long time ago, but I was ashamed. Since I have Harlem now, I want to be able to help her once in a while. When she goes to high school, there's goin' to be times when I'm goin' to be expected to fill some papers out for her. I don't want to embarrass her," Brady said.

Sara held Brady's hand and said, "Harlem thinks the world of you. She is so proud of you. You could never embarrass her. We can start tomorrow if you want to."

Brady said, "Thank you Sara for bein' so understandin' and not ashamed of me."

Sara said, "You say that "a" word again, I'm going to have to throw you off of this porch Brady O'Brannan."

"Thank you again Sara. I guess we better go in and see what the girls are doin'."

The next day Brady got a call from Manny from New York. He said there was a ten thousand dollar reward for the capture of Angelo Risutti and the money was going to Harlem and Coop to divide evenly. He said the check would be coming in a few days.

Brady talked to Harlem right after the phone call. He felt it was up to her to do with the money as she pleased. He thought maybe she would put it away for college.

When Brady told Harlem about the ten thousand dollars, she wanted to give her five thousand dollars to Miss Lucille to rebuild her restaurant. Coop would be out of work for quite a while and his five thousand dollars from the reward would really come in handy to support his family. Harlem told Brady that she would sell the broach Mr. Abermann gave her when the time came in order to go to college. That is what Mr. Abermann wanted her to do with that broach, according to his letter, in case she had no money saved for college.

Brady had a feeling things would go that way because Harlem cared for others more than she cared for herself. He was fine with it. Miss Lucille was more than grateful. Once Miss Lucille rebuilt her restaurant, she made Coop the manager. So everything turned out well for Miss Lucille and Coop.

Harlem went back to school within the next couple of days. She had no trouble getting back in the groove of doing regular school work again. And again, she had the highest test scores in the fifth and sixth grade. Her classmates seemed friendlier to her than they were before she was shot. The girls that ignored her before came up and talked to her now and even included her in on games that were played outside during recess. But, of course, they also started to include Velma in these games. It seemed as though they had an appreciation they never had before for both Harlem and Velma.

A week before May Day, the winners were announced that won king and queen of the May Day. Harlem Rose O'Brannan was voted queen of the May Day. Harlem was shocked. She couldn't believe it. She felt like she was part of something for the first time since she started going to school at Kolter Elementary. These kids really liked her and accepted her. This was something she never thought would never happen in this school. Harlem got to choose the girls for her court. Her first choice was Velma. Velma was so excited she could hardly stand herself. Beautiful gowns were sewn for the event by some of the mothers that could sew. The most beautiful gown was for Harlem, and she made the prettiest queen that the students of Kolter Elementary ever chose.

May Day came and the court walked onto the field towards the maypole first. The gowns were lovely and flowing as the girls walked on the field. There were crowds of people on the field to watch the event that day. Coop and his wife stood proud as they watched Velma walk out on the field. Each girl carried a basket of rose petals and dropped them as they walked. The king and queen were last. Harlem looked beautiful. Brady was so proud as he looked on at his little girl and said, "that's my granddaughter. Her name is Harlem."

chapter 34

THE YEAR IS 1974, graduation night at West Virginia Medical College. The graduation class has one hundred and fifty medical students graduating from medical college. The next step for these new doctors is residency in a hospital. Harlem is sitting on the stage looking down into the audience. The whole first row is her family. She looks at each face and remembers how that person contributed to her life years ago and her life today. Harlem smiles at each face as she glances at these wonderful people that helped her become the woman and doctor she always wanted to be.

Harlem glances at Grandpa Brady. He is still as handsome as ever. He did finally cut his hair, just for this special occasion. He gave Harlem focus in her life to never put out that fire burning in her heart. He taught her to be a strong woman and honest and to stand by her beliefs, no matter what conflict stood in her way, and to never give up. He worked twice as hard selling timber to put her through medical school, because he had such faith in this child that came into his life as a little girl, and now is a woman. She can finally pay him back by making him extra proud of her on this day.

Sara, beautiful and so delicate but so smart. Sara was the mother Harlem needed at a special time in her life when she really needed a woman to guide her and answer her questions. Sara and Grandpa were always there for Harlem for anything she needed. They both were an extra ear to listen to her pre-teen and teenage problems, and they gave her advice whether she wanted it or not. She respected them and listened.

Boone, so funny and so full of life. He not only was Grandpa Brady's best friend but he was also her best friend. Sometimes he doesn't know where he is or who she is. He suffers from Alzheimer's. But it's the moments she savors when he does know who she is. At those times, he remembers every part of her life since she came into his. He saved her life years ago along with her dog Blue Boy. Blue Boy left this earth five years ago and it broke everyone's heart. Blue Boy lived a long happy life and he was also such a dear friend to Harlem.

Manny, the first man of Puerto Rican descent to become Captain of the New York City Crime Unit. He was there for Harlem when her mother died. He never allowed her to be thrown into a place where she would be abused and not loved. He took her to the place where he first found love and compassion, St. Anthony's. He helped find her grandfather, Brady O'Brannan. If he hadn't found Brady, where would she be today? Her life would be totally different. He was there for Brady and her when she was shot. He arrested the criminal that shot her and his accomplice. He is now married with a family of his own and a very frequent visitor to Kolter.

Principal Blackwater, or rather Sheriff Blackwater allowed Harlem to go to his school knowing he could lose his job. He stood up for the rights of everyone. He was Harvard educated and could have been a lawyer but chose to live in the town where his forefathers, the Cherokee Indians, lived. He was the first Cherokee Indian to serve as sheriff in the town of Kolter. It was with honor, respect, trust and dignity that he served as sheriff.

As Harlem felt the cross in her hands that she made for Sister Delores many Christmas' ago, she remembered that Sister Delores always wanted to be there when Harlem graduated from medical school. Well it was never meant to be. That terrible cough she had was the beginning of tuberculosis. It seems like Dr. Hanson was right. She should have gotten that cough checked out but it was too late. She died three years after Harlem left the convent. She gave so much to Harlem when Harlem's world was so dark after her mother died. She stood up for her convictions especially when it came to what was good and right for Harlem. She gave Manny her Bible before she died and in it was the beautiful cross that Harlem was now holding in her hands. She wanted

Harlem to have it whenever she graduated from Medical School so that she could feel that she was with her on her special day.

Velma Little, her special friend in Kolter, was in the front row also with her new husband. It seems like Velma got the last laugh. That chubby little girl grew up to be a beautiful woman. She was crowned Kolter County Queen at the fair two years in a row. She remained Harlem's closest friend throughout the years.

Of course Harlem couldn't forget Mr. Abermann. As her hand brushed across her shoulder, she felt that beautiful broach he gave her on that first Christmas at the convent. He passed away soon after that. She always cherished the letter he wrote to her. He must be very proud of her today because he wanted her to follow that dream of becoming a doctor.

Her mother – Belinda was her greatest inspiration in her life. She believed a person could achieve anything in life as long as they pursued their education and worked hard. And if you have to work and go to school, put your heart into whatever you want to excel in and go for it. All of the good in Harlem's life was instilled in her by her mother. Harlem had a great role model to look up to. This is where Harlem got her start. Her mother was taken away too early in Harlem's life. But thankfully, those that followed in raising Harlem did not fall far from that inspiring tree. Her mother and father were with her in spirit. She could feel it.

The speaker announces, "DOCTOR HARLEM ROSE O'BRANNAN please step up to receive your degree. Congratulations. Doctor O'Brannan is also receiving an award for EXCELLENCE IN MEDICINE."

Harlem shakes hands and the audience applauds loudly, but they are overshadowed by that whole first row- HER FAMILY.

CONGRATULATIONS HARLEM – WELL DONE!!!

Made in the USA
Middletown, DE
23 July 2022